成
为
更
好
的
人

BOB
DYLAN
THE LYRICS 1961–2012
鲍勃·迪伦诗歌集

帝国滑稽剧

[美] 鲍勃·迪伦　著

厄土　李皖　陈震　译

GUANGXI NORMAL UNIVERSITY PRESS
广西师范大学出版社
·桂林·

DIGUO HUAJI JU

LYRICS: 1961-2012
Copyright © 2016, Bob Dylan
All rights reserved.
著作权合同登记号桂图登字:20-2017-053 号

图书在版编目(CIP)数据

鲍勃·迪伦诗歌集:1961—2012. 帝国滑稽剧:汉
英对照 /(美)鲍勃·迪伦著;厄土,李皖,陈震译.
桂林:广西师范大学出版社,2017.6(2019.6 重印)
书名原文:LYRICS:1961-2012
ISBN 978-7-5495-9689-8

Ⅰ. ①鲍… Ⅱ. ①鲍…②厄…③李…④陈…
Ⅲ. ①诗集-美国-现代-汉、英 Ⅳ. ①I712.25

中国版本图书馆 CIP 数据核字(2017)第 078983 号

出　版:广西师范大学出版社
　　　　广西桂林市五里店路9号　邮政编码:541004
网　址:http://www.bbtpress.com
出版人:张艺兵
发　行:广西师范大学出版社
　　　　电话:(0773)2802178
印　刷:山东临沂新华印刷物流集团有限责任公司印刷
　　　　山东临沂高新技术产业开发区新华路
　　　　邮政编码:276017
开　本:740 mm × 1 092 mm　1/32
印　张:8.125　　　字数:87 千字
版　次:2017 年 6 月第 1 版　　2019 年 6 月第 4 次
定　价:25.00 元

如发现印装质量问题,影响阅读,请与出版社发行部门联系调换

目录

得救

来一针爱

异教徒

附加歌词

帝国滑稽剧

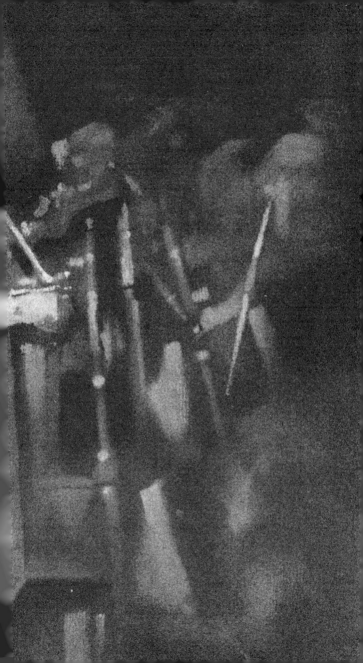

like a poor fool in his prime/trying to read your portrait
you can hear me talk

is your heart made of stone/
                              or solid rock?

得救
Saved

厄土 译

　　发行于 1980 年 6 月的《得救》，是鲍勃·迪伦的第二十张专辑，也是他"基督教三部曲"的第二部，共收录了九首歌曲。

　　那段时期，犹太裔的迪伦深受基督教教义的影响，并宣布自己成为一名基督徒。他甚至在巡演前加入了祈祷仪式，在演出中也增加了不少福音歌曲的表演。

　　这张专辑直观地表现了迪伦彼时对信仰的狂热，歌词中充满了大量直白的《圣经》引文以及显而易见的宗教训词。其中诸如《得救》《预备好了吗？》等歌曲，明显反映出迪伦对《新约·启示录》中末世论的信奉。然而此张专辑浓厚的宗教色彩并不为大众所理解接受，且给迪伦招致了许多非议。另外，专辑销量不佳也令他陷入了事业的低谷。

厄土

得救

（与蒂姆 · 德拉蒙德合作）

我被魔鬼蒙蔽

生来就已败坏

当我走出母腹

便是冰冷如石的尸体

因他的恩典，我被触摸了

因他的言语，我被治愈了

因他的手掌，我被搭救了

因他的灵，我领受了印记

我得救了

因这羔羊的血 [1]

得救了

因这羔羊的血

得救了

得救了

1.《新约 · 彼得前书》1:18-19："知道你们得赎……乃是凭着基督的宝血，如同无瑕疵、无玷污的羔羊之血。" 注释凡涉《圣经》处，译文一律引自和合本，供大致的参照；《圣经》中屡见者，一般仅引一条。

我如此喜乐

是啊，我如此喜乐

我是如此的喜乐

如此喜乐

我想感谢你，上主

我只想感谢你，上主

感谢你，上主

因他的真理，我得称公义

因他的力量，我足堪忍耐

因他的权柄，我得以升举

在他的爱中，我无忧无虑

他用重价赎买了我

使我脱离深坑

那里充满虚空和忿怒

燃烧着熊熊烈火

我得救了

因这羔羊的血

得救了

因这羔羊的血

得救了

得救了

我如此喜乐

是啊，我如此喜乐

我是如此的喜乐

如此喜乐

我想感谢你，上主

我只想感谢你，上主

感谢你，上主

没有人拯救我

没有人敢

在我最后的坠落中

他的仁慈保全了我

不是出于行为

而是因对他的信心，他曾呼召

我受阻太久了

我耽搁太久了

我得救了

因这羔羊的血

得救了

因这羔羊的血

得救了

得救了

我如此喜乐

是啊，我如此喜乐

我是如此的喜乐

如此喜乐

我想感谢你，上主

我只想感谢你，上主

感谢你，上主

Saved
(with Tim Drummond)

I was blinded by the devil
Born already ruined
Stone-cold dead
As I stepped out of the womb
By His grace I have been touched
By His word I have been healed
By His hand I've been delivered
By His spirit I've been sealed

I've been saved
By the blood of the lamb
Saved
By the blood of the lamb
Saved
Saved
And I'm so glad
Yes, I'm so glad
I'm so glad
So glad
I want to thank You, Lord
I just want to thank You, Lord
Thank You, Lord

By His truth I can be upright
By His strength I do endure
By His power I've been lifted
In His love I am secure

He bought me with a price
Freed me from the pit
Full of emptiness and wrath
And the fire that burns in it

I've been saved
By the blood of the lamb
Saved
By the blood of the lamb
Saved
Saved
And I'm so glad
Yes, I'm so glad
I'm so glad
So glad
I want to thank You, Lord
I just want to thank You, Lord
Thank You, Lord

Nobody to rescue me
Nobody would dare
I was going down for the last time
But by His mercy I've been spared
Not by works
But by faith in Him who called
For so long I've been hindered
For so long I've been stalled

I've been saved
By the blood of the lamb
Saved
By the blood of the lamb
Saved

Saved
And I'm so glad
Yes, I'm so glad
I'm so glad
So glad
I want to thank You, Lord
I just want to thank You, Lord
Thank You, Lord

立誓的女人 [1]

立誓的女人和上主订了约
去到那里，她的赏报将是极大的
立誓的女人，闪耀如一颗晨星
我知道我能信赖你，留在你身边

我只想告诉你
我真的想要
比任何朋友都更亲近你
我只想再次
感谢你
因你为我的祈祷
上达于天
我对你，一直，满怀感激
我将永远感激你

我曾经残缺，破碎像一只空杯
我一直等待着上主重建我，充满我

---

1. 通常被认为是美国黑人演员玛丽·爱丽丝·阿提斯（Mary Alice Artes），
她与迪伦在 1979 年前后的恋情推动了迪伦信奉基督教。

我知道他一定会这么做，因他是诚信真实的

他必是爱我甚深，才会为我差遣像你这样好的人

我只想告诉你

我真的想要

比任何朋友都更亲近你

我只想再次

感谢你

因你为我的祈祷

上达于天

我对你，一直，满怀感激

我将永远感激你

立誓的女人，亲密的小女孩

你知晓我隐匿于世最幽深的秘密

你明白，在这经行的大地上我们都是异乡人

我会常伴在你身边，我也立下了誓言

我只想告诉你

我真的想要

比任何朋友都更亲近你

我只想再次

感谢你

因你为我的祈祷

上达于天

我对你，一直，满怀感激

我将永远感激你

Covenant Woman

Covenant woman got a contract with the Lord
Way up yonder, great will be her reward
Covenant woman, shining like a morning star
I know I can trust you to stay where you are

And I just got to tell you
I do intend
To stay closer than any friend
I just got to thank you
Once again
For making your prayers known
Unto heaven for me
And to you, always, so grateful
I will forever be

I've been broken, shattered like an empty cup
I'm just waiting on the Lord to rebuild and fill me up
And I know He will do it 'cause He's faithful and He's true
He must have loved me so much to send me someone
    as fine as you

And I just got to tell you
I do intend
To stay closer than any friend
I just got to thank you
Once again
For making your prayers known
Unto heaven for me
And to you, always, so grateful

I will forever be

Covenant woman, intimate little girl
Who knows those most secret things of me that are hidden
    from the world
You know we are strangers in a land we're passing through
I'll always be right by your side, I've got a covenant too

And I just got to tell you
I do intend
To stay closer than any friend
I just got to thank you
Once again
For making your prayers known
Unto heaven for me
And to you, always, so grateful
I will forever be

我能为你做些什么?

你给了我一切
我能为你做些什么?
你给了我双眼来看见
我能为你做些什么?

你使我摆脱奴役，让我的内心得获新生
你喂饱了一个常常遭拒的饿汉
你打开了没人能关上的门，这门敞开如此宽阔
你拣选我成为少数人的一员
我能为你做些什么?

你为我舍弃了生命
我能为你做些什么?
你为我解答了所有的谜
我能为你做些什么?

凡人一旦出生，你就知道火星已开始飞腾 [1]
他自以为有智慧，注定信从虚谎

1.《旧约·约伯记》5:7："人生在世必遇患难，如同火星飞腾。"

谁能从命中注定的死亡里救他脱离？

哦，你已尽数施为，没人能够冒充

我能为你做些什么？

你已给了一切能给的

我能为你做些什么？

你已给了我生命

我怎样才能为你而活？

我知道有关毒气 [1] 和火箭 [2] 的一切

我不在乎道路如何艰险，告诉我从何处上路

无论你的意旨是什么，让它铭记在我的心田

哦，我配不上它，但我会坚持始终

我能为你做些什么？

1.《新约·雅各书》3:8："惟独舌头没有人能制伏，是不止息的恶物，满了害死人的毒气。"

2.《新约·以弗所书》6:16："此外又拿着信德当作藤牌，可以灭尽那恶者一切的火箭。"

What Can I Do for You?

You have given everything to me
What can I do for You?
You have given me eyes to see
What can I do for You?

Pulled me out of bondage and You made me renewed inside
Filled up a hunger that had always been denied
Opened up a door no man can shut and You opened it up
　　so wide
And You've chosen me to be among the few
What can I do for You?

You have laid down Your life for me
What can I do for You?
You have explained every mystery
What can I do for You?

Soon as a man is born, you know the sparks begin to fly
He gets wise in his own eyes and he's made to believe a lie
Who would deliver him from the death he's bound to die?
Well, You've done it all and there's no more anyone can
　　pretend to do
What can I do for You?

You have given all there is to give
What can I do for You?
You have given me life to live
How can I live for You?

I know all about poison, I know all about fiery darts
I don't care how rough the road is, show me where it starts
Whatever pleases You, tell it to my heart
Well, I don't deserve it but I sure did make it through
What can I do for You?

坚固磐石

哦，我正努力抓牢一块坚固磐石
它先于这世界的根基而成
我不会松手，不能松手，不会松手
我不能松手，不会松手，丝毫也不能松手

他为我而受严惩，他为我而被憎恶
他为了我而被自己所造的世界厌弃
外邦愤怒，或被诅咒
人们在期待虚假的和平到来

哦，我正努力抓牢一块坚固磐石
它先于这世界的根基而成
我不会松手，不能松手，不会松手
我不能松手，不会松手，丝毫也不能松手

这是肉身向灵魂开战的方式
一天二十四小时你都能感受它、听到它
穷尽日光之下的所有手段
在战争分出胜负前他绝不会放弃

哦，我正努力抓牢一块坚固磐石

它先于这世界的根基而成

我不会松手，不能松手，不会松手

我不能松手，不会松手，丝毫也不能松手

Solid Rock

Well, I'm hangin' on to a solid rock
Made before the foundation of the world
And I won't let go, and I can't let go, won't let go
And I can't let go, won't let go and I can't let go no more

For me He was chastised, for me He was hated
For me He was rejected by a world that He created
Nations are angry, cursed are some
People are expecting a false peace to come

Well, I'm hangin' on to a solid rock
Made before the foundation of the world
And I won't let go and I can't let go, won't let go
And I can't let go, won't let go and I can't let go no more

It's the ways of the flesh to war against the spirit
Twenty-four hours a day you can feel it and you can hear it
Using all the devices under the sun
And He never give up 'til the battle's lost or won

Well, I'm hangin' on to a solid rock
Made before the foundation of the world
And I won't let go and I can't let go, won't let go
And I can't let go, won't let go and I can't let go no more

奋力向前

哦，我正在奋力向前
是，我正在奋力向前
哦，我正在奋力向前
向着我主更高的呼召

众人试图阻止我，动摇我的思想
他们说："向我证明他是主，给我显个神迹"
他们需要怎样的神迹？当一切都源自内心
当失去的都已寻回，将临的也已来临

哦，我正在奋力向前
是，我正在奋力向前
哦，我正在奋力向前
向着我主更高的呼召

跺去你脚上的尘土 [1]，不可回头看 [2]

1.《新约·马太福音》10:14："凡不接待你们、不听你们话的人，你们离开那
家或是那城的时候，就把脚上的尘土跺下去。"
2.《旧约·创世记》19:17-26，所多玛被毁前夕，两个天使指引义人罗得一
家逃出城外后不可回头看。城毁时，罗得的妻子回望而变成盐柱。

如今没什么能击倒你，你已一无所缺
诱惑绝非易事，亚当曾被魔鬼支配
因他的罪我无从选择，它流淌在我血管里

哦，我正在奋力向前
是，我正在奋力向前
哦，我正在奋力向前
向着我主更高的呼召

Pressing On

Well I'm pressing on
Yes, I'm pressing on
Well I'm pressing on
To the higher calling of my Lord

Many try to stop me, shake me up in my mind
Say, "Prove to me that He is Lord, show me a sign"
What kind of sign they need when it all come from within
When what's lost has been found, what's to come has
    already been?

Well I'm pressing on
Yes, I'm pressing on
Well I'm pressing on
To the higher calling of my Lord

Shake the dust off of your feet, don't look back
Nothing now can hold you down, nothing that you lack
Temptation's not an easy thing, Adam given the devil reign
Because he sinned I got no choice, it run in my vein

Well I'm pressing on
Yes, I'm pressing on
Well I'm pressing on
To the higher calling of my Lord

在园中 [1]

当他们来园中找他时，他们明白吗？

当他们来园中找他时，他们明白吗？

他们是否明白他就是上帝之子，他就是主？

他们是否听到他对彼得说，"彼得，收起你的刀"？ [2]

当他们来园中找他时，他们明白吗？

当他们来园中找他时，他们明白吗？

当他在城中对他们讲话，他们听到了吗？

当他在城中对他们讲话，他们听到了吗？

尼哥底母在夜晚到来，所以人们没看到他

他说："主啊，告诉我为何人必须重生" [3]

当他在城中对他们讲话，他们听到了吗？

当他在城中对他们讲话，他们听到了吗？

---

1. 指客西马尼园，耶路撒冷的一个园子。《圣经》中，耶稣在这里被捕。

2.《新约·约翰福音》18:11，耶稣被捕时，门徒彼得为保护耶稣而持刀砍伤了大祭司的仆人马勒古，耶稣对彼得说："收刀入鞘吧！我父所给我的那杯，我岂不可喝呢？"

3.《新约·约翰福音》3:4，犹太人的官员、法利赛人尼哥底母夜访耶稣时，问道："人已经老了，如何能重生呢？"

当他治愈瞎子和瘸子时，他们看到了吗？

当他治愈瞎子和瘸子时，他们看到了吗？

当他说："收起你的床走吧，为何你一定要指摘？

我父能做的事，我也照样可以做"

当他治愈瞎子和瘸子时，他们看到了吗？

当他治愈瞎子和瘸子时，他们看到了吗？

他们公然反对他了吗，他们敢吗？

他们公然反对他了吗，他们敢吗？

众人想让他称王，把冠冕戴在了他头上

为何他却悄悄离开去了一处安静的地方？ [1]

他们公然反对他了吗，他们敢吗？

他们公然反对他了吗，他们敢吗？

当他自死者中复活，他们信了吗？

当他自死者中复活，他们信了吗？

他说："天上地下，一切权柄都归于我"

彼时彼处他们是否明白这权柄价值几何？

当他自死者中复活，他们信了吗？

当他自死者中复活，他们信了吗？

1.《新约·约翰福音》6:15："耶稣既知道众人要来强逼他作王，就独自又退到山上去了。"

In the Garden

When they came for Him in the garden, did they know?
When they came for Him in the garden, did they know?
Did they know He was the Son of God, did they know that
   He was Lord?
Did they hear when He told Peter, "Peter, put up your
   sword"?
When they came for Him in the garden, did they know?
When they came for Him in the garden, did they know?

When He spoke to them in the city, did they hear?
When He spoke to them in the city, did they hear?
Nicodemus came at night so he wouldn't be seen by men
Saying, "Master, tell me why a man must be born again"
When He spoke to them in the city, did they hear?
When He spoke to them in the city, did they hear?

When He healed the blind and crippled, did they see?
When He healed the blind and crippled, did they see?
When He said, "Pick up your bed and walk, why must you
   criticize?
Same thing My Father do, I can do likewise"
When He healed the blind and crippled, did they see?
When He healed the blind and crippled, did they see?

Did they speak out against Him, did they dare?
Did they speak out against Him, did they dare?
The multitude wanted to make Him king, put a crown
   upon His head
Why did He slip away to a quiet place instead?

Did they speak out against Him, did they dare?
Did they speak out against Him, did they dare?

When He rose from the dead, did they believe?
When He rose from the dead, did they believe?
He said, "All power is given to Me in heaven and on earth"
Did they know right then and there what the power was
    worth?
When He rose from the dead, did they believe?
When He rose from the dead, did they believe?

救恩

如果你在内心寻到了它，我会被原谅吗？

我想我欠你个道歉

我许多次逃离死亡，我明白我活着

唯赖我所蒙的救恩

那时我曾有过一个念头，我会

永远沉睡在松木盒子里

我的信仰支撑我活着，但我仍旧会流泪

为我所蒙的救恩

哦，生命死去，然后复活来临

无论我会去向何处，我都乐于接受

我全然信靠他，我唯一的庇佑

就是我所蒙的救恩

哦，恶魔那闪耀的光芒，它可以是最令人目眩的[1]

但是去寻找爱吧，这些都不过是虚荣

1.《新约·哥林多后书》11:14："这也不足为怪，因为连撒但（即撒旦）也装作光明的天使。"

当我环顾世界，我所追寻的一切
就是我所蒙的救恩

恶人都不知道平安，而你也不能佯装
只存在一条路，它通向髑髅地[1]
有时它令人沮丧，但我知道自己能坚持到底
唯赖我所蒙的救恩

---

1. 髑髅地，《圣经》中的耶稣受难地。

Saving Grace

If you find it in Your heart, can I be forgiven?
Guess I owe You some kind of apology
I've escaped death so many times, I know I'm only living
By the saving grace that's over me

By this time I'd-a thought I would be sleeping
In a pine box for all eternity
My faith keeps me alive, but I still be weeping
For the saving grace that's over me

Well, the death of life, then come the resurrection
Wherever I am welcome is where I'll be
I put all my confidence in Him, my sole protection
Is the saving grace that's over me

Well, the devil's shining light, it can be most blinding
But to search for love, that ain't no more than vanity
As I look around this world all that I'm finding
Is the saving grace that's over me

The wicked know no peace and you just can't fake it
There's only one road and it leads to Calvary
It gets discouraging at times, but I know I'll make it
By the saving grace that's over me

预备好了吗？

预备好了吗，预备好了吗？
预备好了吗，预备好了吗？

预备好去见耶稣了吗？
去你应该去的地方了吗？
当他看到你，他会认得你吗
抑或他会说，"离开我"？[1]

预备好了吗，愿你已预备妥当
我预备好了吗，我预备好了吗？
我预备好了吗，我预备好了吗？

是否我已预备好为弟兄舍命
背起自己的十字架？
是否我已顺服于上帝的旨意
还是依旧表现得像是主宰？

1.《新约·马太福音》7:21，耶稣说："我就明明地告诉他们说：'我从来不认识你们，你们这些作恶的人，离开我去吧！'"

我预备好了吗，愿我已预备妥当

当毁灭迅速降临
来不及去道永别
是否你已拿定主意
想去天堂还是地狱？

预备好了吗，预备好了吗？

是否你还有未了之事？
是否还有什么牵挂着你？
是否你正在为自己着想
还是你要随波逐流？

预备好了吗，愿你已预备妥当
预备好了吗？

预备好接受审判了吗？
预备好面对可怖的利刃了吗？[1]

1.《旧约·以赛亚书》27:1："到那日，耶和华必用他刚硬有力的大刀刑罚鳄鱼，就是那快行的蛇……"

预备好面对哈米吉多顿[1]了吗？

预备好迎接主的日子了吗？

预备好了吗，我愿你已预备妥当

---

1. 哈米吉多顿，指末日的善恶决战，见《新约·启示录》16:13-16。

Are You Ready?

Are you ready, are you ready?
Are you ready, are you ready?

Are you ready to meet Jesus?
Are you where you ought to be?
Will He know you when He sees you
Or will He say, "Depart from Me"?

Are you ready, hope you're ready
Am I ready, am I ready?
Am I ready, am I ready?

Am I ready to lay down my life for the brethren
And to take up my cross?
Have I surrendered to the will of God
Or am I still acting like the boss?

Am I ready, hope I'm ready

When destruction cometh swiftly
And there's no time to say a fare-thee-well
Have you decided whether you want to be
In heaven or in hell?

Are you ready, are you ready?

Have you got some unfinished business?
Is there something holding you back?
Are you thinking for yourself

Or are you following the pack?

Are you ready, hope you're ready
Are you ready?

Are you ready for the judgment?
Are you ready for that terrible swift sword?
Are you ready for Armageddon?
Are you ready for the day of the Lord?

Are you ready, I hope you're ready

黄金之城

那儿有座黄金之城

远离吞噬你灵魂的激烈竞争

远离疯狂和阻拦你的障碍

那儿有座黄金之城

那儿有座光明之城

高耸在天堂，街道明净

荣耀归于主——并非因为行为或势力[1]

那儿有座光明之城

那儿有座爱之城

被天上的群星和权柄簇拥

远离这个世界和构成梦的材料[2]

那儿有座爱之城

1.《新约·撒迦利亚书》4:6，提到"不是倚靠势力，不是倚靠才能，乃是倚靠我的灵方能成事"。

2. 源自美国演员亨弗莱·鲍嘉主演的电影《马耳他之鹰》（*The Maltese Falcon*，1941）中的台词："这是构成梦的材料。"这句源出莎士比亚的戏剧《暴风雨》第四幕第一场的台词："构成我们的料子也就是那梦幻的料子……"（朱生豪译文）

那儿有座恩典之城

你在圣所里汲饮圣水

没有人害怕展露自己的面容 [1]

在那恩典之城

那儿有座平安之城

所有沉沦的恶行都已消停

英雄已然仆倒 [2]，也没有警察

那儿有座平安之城

那儿有座希望之城

在幽谷之上，洒满阳光的葱翠山坡

我只需要一把斧头和一根绳索

前往那希望之城

我正奔赴那黄金之城

趁为时未晚，趁天未转寒

趁我尚未疲倦，趁我未至衰年

我正奔赴那黄金之城

1.《旧约·创世记》3:8-10，违令吃禁果后的亚当和夏娃藏了起来，害怕
见上帝。

2.《旧约·撒母耳记下》1:27 有句云："英雄何竟仆倒！战具何竟灭没！"

City of Gold

There is a City of Gold
Far from the rat race that eats at your soul
Far from the madness and the bars that hold
There is a City of Gold

There is a City of Light
Raised up in the heavens and the streets are bright
Glory to God—not by deeds or by might
There is a City of Light

There is a City of Love
Surrounded by stars and the powers above
Far from this world and the stuff dreams are made of
There is a City of Love

There is a City of Grace
You drink holy water in sanctified space
No one is afraid to show their face
In the City of Grace

There is a City of Peace
Where all foul forms of destruction cease
Where the mighty have fallen and there are no police
There is a City of Peace

There is a City of Hope
Above the ravine on the green sunlit slope
All I need is an axe and a rope
To get to the City of Hope

I'm heading for the City of Gold
Before it's too late, before it gets too cold
Before I'm too tired, before I'm too old
I'm heading for the City of Gold

People tell me it's a sin
To know and see too much within
But I still believe she was my twin
I still can feel the string (It was all over everything)
She was born in the Spring, (But I lost the ring)
But I was born too late)
Blame it on a Simple Twist of Fate

来一针爱
Shot of Love

李皖 译（郝佳 校）

《来一针爱》是鲍勃·迪伦的第二十一张录音室专辑，发行于 1981 年 8 月 10 日，被认为是他"基督教三部曲"的最后一部。与富有浓厚福音歌曲色彩的前两部不同，此专辑宗教与世俗题材掺杂，编曲配器根植于摇滚乐。

自迪伦开启"重生／救赎"的主题起，评论界的严厉批评就一直没停过。人们普遍认为，那位敢于挑战传统、撕开文化假面、刺穿政治黑幕的斗士变得怯弱、倒退、迂腐了，龟缩到宗教的陈腐教义中，变为 20 世纪 60 年代自由思想的反动力量。

这张专辑可谓是对此批评的尖锐回击，迪伦一展其所擅长的"吵架模式"，极尽讽刺挖苦之能事，对论敌的虚伪、浅薄和愚蠢予以毫不留情的揭露与驳斥。实际上，迪伦在 20 世纪七八十年代向犹太教、基督教教义的转向，有其深刻的思想脉络。这种转向仍然是投向现实的，是迪伦对时代困境、社会动荡、人生意义等问题的进一步思索。此专辑清晰地反映了迪伦当时的思想走向，虽然起初所得的评价甚低，但随着时间推移，它的价值被不断重估，相关评价也逐渐转为正面。

今天看来，迪伦的反击直指问题根本，颇为有力。他揭示了人们不接受"纯粹的爱"这一真相，呈现了"烦恼"与人生悲凉处境的绝对性，描写出如"沙子"一般的、人类无所归依的彷徨境遇，令人为之深思。此外，隐含着宗教意指的"新郎""加勒比海的风""安吉丽娜""我主与救主"等意象，均充满真实感，富有文学感染力。

李皖

来一针爱

我需要来一针爱，我需要来一针爱

不需要来针海洛因治愈我的病
不需要来针松脂，只会让我双膝跪地
不需要来针可待因让我懊悔
不需要来瓶威士忌，让我当上总统

我需要来一针爱，我需要来一针爱

医生，听到没有？我需要医疗救助
我看到这世上的万国 [1] 这让我恐惧
我得的病不疼，只是会要我的命
像追随耶稣的人，当他们给他的首级定了价 [2]

我需要来一针爱，我需要来一针爱

1.《新约·马太福音》4:8，魔鬼试探耶稣，"将世上的万国与万国的荣华都指给他看"。
2.《新约·马太福音》26:15，犹大出卖耶稣，得到三十块钱。

我才不需要什么不在场证据，既然和你在一起
我听到的全部谣言你一样也听到了
不要给我放电影也不要给我书看
这治不了内伤也戒不掉毒瘾

我需要来一针爱，我需要来一针爱

为什么我要取你性命？
你只是谋杀了我父亲，强奸了他妻子
用毒笔[1]给我的孩子们文身
嘲笑我的神，羞辱我的朋友

我需要来一针爱，我需要来一针爱

今夜我不想和人待一块儿
维罗妮卡无踪影，梅维丝又不合适
有一个恨我的男人他敏捷、麻利，就在附近
难道我该耽搁下去等他到来？

我需要来一针爱，我需要来一针爱

---

1. 毒笔，又指恶意中伤的匿名信。

今夜是什么让那风呼啸?
甚至懒得过马路，我的车也动作古怪
打了个电话回家，每个人似乎都已搬走
我的良心今天开始来骚扰我

我需要来一针爱，我需要来一针爱

我需要来一针爱，我需要来一针爱
如果你是医生，给我来一针爱吧

Shot of Love

I need a shot of love, I need a shot of love

Don't need a shot of heroin to kill my disease
Don't need a shot of turpentine, only bring me to my knees
Don't need a shot of codeine to help me to repent
Don't need a shot of whiskey, help me be president

I need a shot of love, I need a shot of love

Doctor, can you hear me? I need some Medicaid
I seen the kingdoms of the world and it's makin' me feel
    afraid
What I got ain't painful, it's just bound to kill me dead
Like the men that followed Jesus when they put a price
    upon His head

I need a shot of love, I need a shot of love

I don't need no alibi when I'm spending time with you
I've heard all of them rumors and you have heard 'em too
Don't show me no picture show or give me no book to read
It don't satisfy the hurt inside nor the habit that it feeds

I need a shot of love, I need a shot of love

Why would I want to take your life?
You've only murdered my father, raped his wife
Tattooed my babies with a poison pen
Mocked my God, humiliated my friends

I need a shot of love, I need a shot of love

Don't wanna be with nobody tonight
Veronica not around nowhere, Mavis just ain't right
There's a man that hates me and he's swift, smooth and near
Am I supposed to set back and wait until he's here?

I need a shot of love, I need a shot of love

What makes the wind wanna blow tonight?
Don't even feel like crossing the street and my car ain't
    actin' right
Called home, everybody seemed to have moved away
My conscience is beginning to bother me today

I need a shot of love, I need a shot of love

I need a shot of love, I need a shot of love
If you're a doctor, I need a shot of love

我的一颗心

我的一颗心请你安静
你可以玩火但是你要付出代价
不要让她知道
不要让她知道你爱她
不要当傻瓜，不要眼睁睁
我的一颗心啊

我的一颗心请快回家
没理由再浪荡，没理由再溜达
不要让她看到
不要让她看到你需要她
不要让自己过线
我的一颗心啊

我的一颗心快回到原来地方
这只会添乱如果你让她进来
不要让她听到
不要让她听到你想要她
不要让她以为你认为她很好
我的一颗心啊

我的一颗心你知道她从来不真心

她只会把从你这儿弄到的爱给别人

不要让她知道

不要让她知道你去哪儿

不要解开那系好的结

我的一颗心啊

我的一颗心如此恶毒充满狡诈

给你一寸你将进一里

不要让自己摔倒

不要让自己失足

如果你不愿坐牢，就不要去犯罪

我的一颗心啊

Heart of Mine

Heart of mine be still
You can play with fire but you'll get the bill
Don't let her know
Don't let her know that you love her
Don't be a fool, don't be blind
Heart of mine

Heart of mine go back home
You got no reason to wander, you got no reason to roam
Don't let her see
Don't let her see that you need her
Don't put yourself over the line
Heart of mine

Heart of mine go back where you been
It'll only be trouble for you if you let her in
Don't let her hear
Don't let her hear you want her
Don't let her think you think she's fine
Heart of mine

Heart of mine you know that she'll never be true
She'll only give to others the love that she's gotten from you
Don't let her know
Don't let her know where you're going
Don't untie the ties that bind
Heart of mine

Heart of mine so malicious and so full of guile

Give you an inch and you'll take a mile
Don't let yourself fall
Don't let yourself stumble
If you can't do the time, don't do the crime
Heart of mine

耶稣名下所有

好吧来谈谈他吧因为他让你有疑虑
因为他摒绝了你离了就活不下去的东西
像其他人那样在背后嘲笑他吧
当他走过时，提醒他自己以前是什么样子

他是耶稣名下所有
你恨他恨得入骨
你有那更好的
你有那铁石之心

当他从街上走过时，你停下了话头
希望他自己摔一跤，啊，那该有多美
因为他再不会被迷信利用
因为他不会被你们所崇拜的贿赂或收买

他是耶稣名下所有
你恨他恨得入骨
你有那更好的
你有那铁石之心

那使你规矩的鞭子却不会让他跳起
就说他笨耳朵，就说他木脑壳
你想试下他的胆量，就说他不切实际
因为他不向你伺候的国君进贡

他是耶稣名下所有
你恨他恨得入骨
你有那更好的
你有那铁石之心

说他是个失败者因为他毫无常识
因为他不为了利己而损人
因为他不怕尝试，因为他不看着你微笑
因为他不对你讲笑话或童话，就说他没有风度

他是耶稣名下所有
你恨他恨得入骨
你有那更好的
你有那铁石之心

你可以嘲笑那拯救，你可以参加奥运会
你认为当你长眠时你将回到你所来之处
但你离开子宫后已有了好一段故事，你已经变了

那个真的你发生了什么，你究竟成了谁的俘虏？

他是耶稣名下所有
你恨他恨得入骨
你有那更好的
你有那铁石之心

Property of Jesus

Go ahead and talk about him because he makes you doubt
Because he has denied himself the things that you can't live
    without
Laugh at him behind his back just like the others do
Remind him of what he used to be when he comes walkin'
    through

He's the property of Jesus
Resent him to the bone
You got something better
You've got a heart of stone

Stop your conversation when he passes on the street
Hope he falls upon himself, oh, won't that be sweet
Because he can't be exploited by superstition anymore
Because he can't be bribed or bought by the things that you
    adore

He's the property of Jesus
Resent him to the bone
You got something better
You've got a heart of stone

When the whip that's keeping you in line doesn't make him
    jump
Say he's hard-of-hearin', say that he's a chump
Say he's out of step with reality as you try to test his nerve
Because he doesn't pay no tribute to the king that you serve

He's the property of Jesus
Resent him to the bone
You got something better
You've got a heart of stone

Say that he's a loser 'cause he got no common sense
Because he don't increase his worth at someone else's
    expense
Because he's not afraid of trying, 'cause he don't look at you
    and smile
'Cause he doesn't tell you jokes or fairy tales, say he's got no
    style

He's the property of Jesus
Resent him to the bone
You got something better
You've got a heart of stone

You can laugh at salvation, you can play Olympic games
You think that when you rest at last you'll go back from
    where you came
But you've picked up quite a story and you've changed since
    the womb
What happened to the real you, you've been captured but
    by whom?

He's the property of Jesus
Resent him to the bone
You got something better
You've got a heart of stone

伦尼·布鲁斯 [1]

伦尼·布鲁斯死了但他的灵魂将一直活着

从没得过金球奖，也没去过椴树村 [2]

他是个不法之徒，确实如此

比你做过的不法之徒更名副其实

伦尼·布鲁斯走了但他的精神一直活着

也许他有一些问题，也许有些事他没能解决

但是他确实有意思他确实讲了实话他知道他在说什么

从没有抢劫过教堂或者砍过孩子的头

他只是把大伙儿带到高处，在他们的床上投一束光

他在别的海岸，他不想活下去了

伦尼·布鲁斯死了但他什么恶都没作过

他只是敏锐地揭开了盖子，超前于那个时代

---

1. 伦尼·布鲁斯（Lenny Bruce，1925—1966），美国喜剧演员、社会批评家，因其表演破坏力太强，1964 年被判以"猥亵罪"。2003 年，时任纽约州长乔治·帕塔基（George Pataki）就此予以致歉。
2. 椴树村，又译作"希南农"，原为戒毒康复社区，1958 年在加州成立，有以"讲真话"为名的病患者互相刺激的疗法，后演化为邪教组织，至 1991 年解体。

我和他有一次同乘一辆出租车

只是一英里半的路程，却像走了几个月

伦尼·布鲁斯继续前行，就像杀害他的那些人，死了

他们说他令人恶心因为他不按规矩出牌

其实他只是让人看到他的时代的智者不过是一帮蠢货

他们给他盖印给他贴标签就像出厂的裤子衬衣

他在一个战场上打了场战争那里每一场胜利都令人伤痛

伦尼·布鲁斯够坏，他是你从不曾拥有的兄弟

Lenny Bruce

Lenny Bruce is dead but his ghost lives on and on
Never did get any Golden Globe award, never made it to
　Synanon
He was an outlaw, that's for sure
More of an outlaw than you ever were
Lenny Bruce is gone but his spirit's livin' on and on

Maybe he had some problems, maybe some things that he
　couldn't work out
But he sure was funny and he sure told the truth and he
　knew what he was talkin' about
Never robbed any churches nor cut off any babies' heads
He just took the folks in high places and he shined a light in
　their beds
He's on some other shore, he didn't wanna live anymore

Lenny Bruce is dead but he didn't commit any crime
He just had the insight to rip off the lid before its time
I rode with him in a taxi once
Only for a mile and a half, seemed like it took a couple of
　months
Lenny Bruce moved on and like the ones that killed him,
　gone

They said that he was sick 'cause he didn't play by the rules
He just showed the wise men of his day to be nothing more
　than fools
They stamped him and they labeled him like they do with
　pants and shirts

He fought a war on a battlefield where every victory hurts
Lenny Bruce was bad, he was the brother that you never had

冲淡的爱

纯粹的爱盼望一切

相信一切，不会暗中操纵

不会溜进卧室，高大、黝黑、英俊

俘获你的心，挟持它索要赎金

你不要纯粹的爱

你想把爱溺水里

你想要冲淡的爱

纯粹的爱从无不实之词

只会为你说情，而不是责备你

不会蒙骗，引你入歧途

不会写出来，让你在假供词上签字

你不要纯粹的爱

你想把爱溺水里

你想要冲淡的爱

纯粹的爱不会让你迷路

不会拖后腿，不会搅乱你的日子

不会以愚蠢的愿望腐蚀你，败坏你

不会让你嫉妒，让你疑神疑鬼

你不要纯粹的爱

你想把爱溺水里

你想要冲淡的爱

纯粹的爱不是什么意外

总是按时发生，总是令人满意

一支永恒的火焰，静静燃烧

从不需要张狂[1]，辗转不安渴念

你不要纯粹的爱

你想把爱溺水里

你想要冲淡的爱

1.《新约·哥林多前书》13:4：“爱是不嫉妒，爱是不自夸，不张狂……”

Watered-Down Love

Love that's pure hopes all things
Believes all things, won't pull no strings
Won't sneak up into your room, tall, dark and handsome
Capture your heart and hold it for ransom

You don't want a love that's pure
You wanna drown love
You want a watered-down love

Love that's pure, it don't make no false claims
Intercedes for you 'stead of casting you blame
Will not deceive you or lead you into transgression
Won't write it up and make you sign a false confession

You don't want a love that's pure
You wanna drown love
You want a watered-down love

Love that's pure won't lead you astray
Won't hold you back, won't mess up your day
Won't pervert you, corrupt you with stupid wishes
It don't make you envious, it don't make you suspicious

You don't want a love that's pure
You wanna drown love
You want a watered-down love

Love that's pure ain't no accident
Always on time, is always content

An eternal flame, quietly burning
Never needs to be proud, restlessly yearning

You don't want a love that's pure
You wanna drown love
You want a watered-down love

新郎还在圣坛上苦等 [1]

我在贫民窟祈祷着，脸埋在水泥里
听到拳手的最后一声呻吟，看到无辜的人被血洗
摸索着电灯开关，恶心欲呕
她走过门厅，那四壁已经恶化

约旦河以西，直布罗陀巨岩以东
我看到那页面翻过
新世纪的幕布升起
我看见那新郎还在圣坛上苦等

为努力达到心灵的纯净，他们以抢劫罪逮捕你
把羞怯误会成冷漠，把沉默误会成摆架子
这个早上得到发给我的一条信息
关于那疯狂：成为从来不想成为的那种人

约旦河以西，直布罗陀巨岩以东
我看见舞台烧起来
新世纪的幕布升起

---

1. 基督教中，以新郎喻耶稣基督，以新娘喻教会。

我看见那新郎还在圣坛上苦等

不知道我该怎样谈论克劳德特，她不会再回来纠缠我了
最终我不得不放弃她，大约在她开始想我的时刻
但是我知道上帝垂怜受诽谤和受羞辱的人
为那女人我什么都愿做，要是她不曾让我深感负有义务

约旦河以西，直布罗陀巨岩以东
我看见牢房烧起来
新世纪的幕布升起
我看见那新郎还在圣坛上苦等

用你的手摸摸我的头，宝贝，我是不是在发烧？
我看见那些本应该更明白的人像家具般干站着
在你和你想要的东西之间有一堵墙你要跃过
今夜你有了力量去得到，明天你不会还有力量拥有

约旦河以西，直布罗陀巨岩以东
我看见舞台烧起来
新世纪的幕布升起
我看见那新郎还在圣坛上苦等

城市着火了，电话失灵

他们在屠杀修女和士兵，边境战争爆发

我该怎样谈论克劳德特？一月以来我就没见过她

她也许已体面地结婚了，也许在布宜诺斯艾利斯开窑子

约旦河以西，直布罗陀巨岩以东

我看见舞台烧起来

新世纪的幕布升起

我看见那新郎还在圣坛上苦等

The Groom's Still Waiting at the Altar

Prayed in the ghetto with my face in the cement
Heard the last moan of a boxer, seen the massacre of the
    innocent
Felt around for the light switch, became nauseated
She was walking down the hallway while the walls
    deteriorated

West of the Jordan, east of the Rock of Gibraltar
I see the turning of the page
Curtain risin' on a new age
See the groom still waitin' at the altar

Try to be pure at heart, they arrest you for robbery
Mistake your shyness for aloofness, your silence for snobbery
Got the message this morning, the one that was sent to me
About the madness of becomin' what one was never meant
    to be

West of the Jordan, east of the Rock of Gibraltar
I see the burning of the stage
Curtain risin' on a new age
See the groom still waitin' at the altar

Don't know what I can say about Claudette that wouldn't
    come back to haunt me
Finally had to give her up 'bout the time she began to want
    me
But I know God has mercy on them who are slandered and
    humiliated

I'd a-done anything for that woman if she didn't make me
  feel so obligated

West of the Jordan, east of the Rock of Gibraltar
I see the burning of the cage
Curtain risin' on a new stage
See the groom still waitin' at the altar

Put your hand on my head, baby, do I have a temperature?
I see people who are supposed to know better standin'
  around like furniture
There's a wall between you and what you want and you got
  to leap it
Tonight you got the power to take it, tomorrow you won't
  have the power to keep it

West of the Jordan, east of the Rock of Gibraltar
I see the burning of the stage
Curtain risin' on a new age
See the groom still waitin' at the altar

Cities on fire, phones out of order
They're killing nuns and soldiers, there's fighting on the
  border
What can I say about Claudette? Ain't seen her since
  January
She could be respectfully married or running a whorehouse
  in Buenos Aires

West of the Jordan, east of the Rock of Gibraltar
I see the burning of the stage
Curtain risin' on a new age
See the groom still waitin' at the altar

死人，死人

空洞无聊的话来自邪僻之心 [1]
执着于奇怪的允诺，还没结果就蔫在藤上
永远不能区分好与坏
啊，我再不能忍受，我再不能忍受
这让我感到多么悲伤

死人，死人
你什么时候复活？
你的心结满了蛛网
你的眼睛满是灰尘

撒旦捉着你脚后跟 [2]，你的头发里筑了鸟窝
你到底有没有信仰？你有没有爱要分享？
你拧着头的样子，每个动作都是在诅咒上帝
啊，我再不能忍受，我再不能忍受
你想要证明什么？

1.《新约·罗马书》1:28，"他们既然故意不认识神，神就任凭他们存邪僻的心，行那些不合理的事……"
2.《旧约·创世记》3:15，耶和华对引诱夏娃吃禁果的蛇说："女人的后裔要伤你的头，你要伤他的脚跟。"

死人，死人

你什么时候复活？

你的心结满了蛛网

你的眼睛满是灰尘

诱惑力、花花世界和罪恶政治

你为我造的贫民窟也是你最后的栖息之地

引擎空转支配了你的心

啊，我再不能忍受，我再不能忍受

假装你是如此聪明伶俐

死人，死人

你什么时候复活？

你的心结满了蛛网

你的眼睛满是灰尘

你想用什么制服我，教义还是枪？

我的背已顶着墙，我还能逃到哪去？

你穿着小礼服，翻领上戴着花

啊，我再不能忍受，我再不能忍受

你想要把我拖进地狱

死人，死人

你什么时候复活？

你的心结满了蛛网

你的眼睛满是灰尘

Dead Man, Dead Man

Uttering idle words from a reprobate mind
Clinging to strange promises, dying on the vine
Never bein' able to separate the good from the bad
Ooh, I can't stand it, I can't stand it
It's makin' me feel so sad

Dead man, dead man
When will you arise?
Cobwebs in your mind
Dust upon your eyes

Satan got you by the heel, there's a bird's nest in your hair
Do you have any faith at all? Do you have any love to share?
The way that you hold your head, cursin' God with every
    move
Ooh, I can't stand it, I can't stand it
What are you tryin' to prove?

Dead man, dead man
When will you arise?
Cobwebs in your mind
Dust upon your eyes

The glamour and the bright lights and the politics of sin
The ghetto that you build for me is the one you end up in
The race of the engine that overrules your heart
Ooh, I can't stand it, I can't stand it
Pretending that you're so smart

Dead man, dead man
When will you arise?
Cobwebs in your mind
Dust upon your eyes

What are you tryin' to overpower me with, the doctrine or
    the gun?
My back is already to the wall, where can I run?
The tuxedo that you're wearin', the flower in your lapel
Ooh, I can't stand it, I can't stand it
You wanna take me down to hell

Dead man, dead man
When will you arise?
Cobwebs in your mind
Dust upon your eyes

在夏季

我已经在你面前一小时左右
还是已有一天？我真的不知道
太阳一直未落，而树桠低垂
在那柔和而灿烂的大海边
你是否为我的所作所为感到钦佩
或者为我不做的，为我所隐藏的？
我是否已失去理智当我试图摆脱
你看到的一切？

在夏季，啊在夏季
在夏季，当你和我在一起

我有这颗心而你有这热血
我们穿过了铁幕我们穿过了泥泞
这时传来了警告洪水要来了
洪水让所有人获得自由
愚人们在嘲笑罪恶
他们试图赢得我们的忠诚
但是你比我的亲人更亲近
当他们不想知道也不想看到

在夏季，啊在夏季

在夏季，当你和我在一起

陌生人，他们插手着我们的事情

贫穷和耻辱是他们的

而所有的苦楚都不能与

将要获得的荣耀比拟

而我依然带着你给我的礼物

它现在变成了我的一部分，受到珍爱和保存

将随我到坟墓

随我到永恒

在夏季，啊在夏季

在夏季，当你和我在一起

In the Summertime

I was in your presence for an hour or so
Or was it a day? I truly don't know
Where the sun never set, where the trees hung low
By that soft and shining sea
Did you respect me for what I did
Or for what I didn't do, or for keeping it hid?
Did I lose my mind when I tried to get rid
Of everything you see?

In the summertime, ah in the summertime
In the summertime, when you were with me

I got the heart and you got the blood
We cut through iron and we cut through mud
Then came the warnin' that was before the flood
That set everybody free
Fools they made a mock of sin
Our loyalty they tried to win
But you were closer to me than my next of kin
When they didn't want to know or see

In the summertime, ah in the summertime
In the summertime when you were with me

Strangers, they meddled in our affairs
Poverty and shame was theirs
But all that sufferin' was not to be compared
With the glory that is to be
And I'm still carrying the gift you gave

It's a part of me now, it's been cherished and saved
It'll be with me unto the grave
And then unto eternity

In the summertime, ah in the summertime
In the summertime when you were with me

烦恼

在城市烦恼，在农场烦恼
你有了幸运符，你有了兔子脚 [1]
但是它们无济于事当有了烦恼

烦恼
烦恼，烦恼，烦恼
没有别的只有烦恼

在水里烦恼，在空中烦恼
一路向前到世界另一侧，你会找到烦恼
革命甚至也不能解决烦恼

烦恼
烦恼，烦恼，烦恼
没有别的只有烦恼

干旱和饥荒，给灵魂打包
迫害，行刑，失控的政府

---

1. 在一些文化中，兔子脚被认为能带来好运。

你可以看到写在墙上的文字 [1] 在邀请烦恼

烦恼
烦恼，烦恼，烦恼
没有别的只有烦恼

把耳朵贴向铁轨，把耳朵贴向地面
你是否觉得你从不是独自一个即使周围空无一人？
从宇宙之初人就受了诅咒，被烦恼

烦恼
烦恼，烦恼，烦恼
没有别的只有烦恼

伤心人夜总会，被诅咒的体育场
立法机关，变态人性，粗暴摔上的门
洞穿那无穷，你看到的一切是烦恼

烦恼

---

1. 写在墙上的文字，指凶兆。《旧约·但以理书》5:5-28，伯沙撒王的宴会上，"忽有人的指头显出，在王宫与灯台相对的墙上写字"，但以理为王解读文字，说神预告了其国的终结。

烦恼，烦恼，烦恼
没有别的只有烦恼

Trouble

Trouble in the city, trouble in the farm
You got your rabbit's foot, you got your good-luck charm
But they can't help you none when there's trouble

Trouble
Trouble, trouble, trouble
Nothin' but trouble

Trouble in the water, trouble in the air
Go all the way to the other side of the world, you'll find
trouble there
Revolution even ain't no solution for trouble

Trouble
Trouble, trouble, trouble
Nothin' but trouble

Drought and starvation, packaging of the soul
Persecution, execution, governments out of control
You can see the writing on the wall inviting trouble

Trouble
Trouble, trouble, trouble
Nothin' but trouble

Put your ear to the train tracks, put your ear to the ground
You ever feel like you're never alone even when there's
nobody else around?

Since the beginning of the universe man's been cursed by
   trouble

Trouble
Trouble, trouble, trouble
Nothin' but trouble

Nightclubs of the broken-hearted, stadiums of the damned
Legislature, perverted nature, doors that are rudely slammed
Look into infinity, all you see is trouble

Trouble
Trouble, trouble, trouble
Nothin' but trouble

每一粒沙子

在我忏悔时，在我最深切渴求的时刻
我脚下的泪池淹没了每一粒新生种子
身体里升起一个垂死的声音它向某处伸展着
爬行在危险中爬行在绝望的道德里

不要有任何反省错误的倾向
就像是该隐[1]，我现在才看到这条必须打破的事件链
在这一刻的暴怒中我能看见主人的手
在每一片战栗的叶子上，在每一粒沙子里[2]

啊，沉溺的花和往昔的野草
就像是罪犯，扼住了良知和欢乐的呼吸
太阳打在时间的台阶上，照亮道路
舒缓那百无聊赖的痛苦和腐朽的记忆

我盯着诱惑的怒火之门廊

---

1. 该隐，在《圣经》中为亚当和夏娃的儿子，第一个杀人者。
2. 以上两行歌词源自威廉·布莱克的诗歌《天真的预兆》（ Auguries of Innocence ）。

每一次当我走过，我都听到自己的名字
继续向前走，我渐渐得以明白
每一根头发都被数过了，[1] 就像每一粒沙子

我从赤贫变成了巨富，在夜的悲哀中
在夏之梦的暴力中，在冬之光的寒冷中
在孤独遁空的苦涩之舞中
在映着每一张遗忘面孔的无辜的破镜中

我听着那远古的脚步就像海洋的运动
我转过身去，有时有人在那儿，有时只有我自己
我对人的本质仍摇摆不定
像是每一只坠落的麻雀，像是每一粒沙子

1.《新约·马太福音》10:30，耶稣说："就是你们的头发也被数过了。"

Every Grain of Sand

In the time of my confession, in the hour of my deepest
 need
When the pool of tears beneath my feet flood every newborn
 seed
There's a dyin' voice within me reaching out somewhere
Toiling in the danger and in the morals of despair

Don't have the inclination to look back on any mistake
Like Cain, I now behold this chain of events that I must
 break
In the fury of the moment I can see the Master's hand
In every leaf that trembles, in every grain of sand

Oh, the flowers of indulgence and the weeds of yesteryear
Like criminals, they have choked the breath of conscience
 and good cheer
The sun beat down upon the steps of time to light the way
To ease the pain of idleness and the memory of decay

I gaze into the doorway of temptation's angry flame
And every time I pass that way I always hear my name
Then onward in my journey I come to understand
That every hair is numbered like every grain of sand

I have gone from rags to riches in the sorrow of the night
In the violence of a summer's dream, in the chill of a wintry
 light
In the bitter dance of loneliness fading into space
In the broken mirror of innocence on each forgotten face

I hear the ancient footsteps like the motion of the sea
Sometimes I turn, there's someone there, other times it's
    only me
I am hanging in the balance of the reality of man
Like every sparrow falling, like every grain of sand

别说出去，这事就你知我知

别说出去，这事就你知我知

这些人在插手我们的事，他们不在我们这边

别说出去，这事就你知我知

在所有的门关上之前，在我们分开之前

他们要拉你反对我，拉我反对你

直到我们不知道该信谁

啊亲爱的，能否别说出去，这事就你知我知？

别说出去，这事就你知我知

我们度过了这么多艰难时刻他们从无分担

从前他们对我们什么都不说

现在却突然好像他们一直在关切

我们需要的是诚实

和一点点谦让及信任

啊亲爱的，能否别说出去，这事就你知我知？

我知道我们不完美

可是话说回来，他们也不完美

他们表现得好像我们必须为他们而活

好像就没有别的法子了

这真是让我有一点儿烦

我们能不能倒回去一点儿
回到醒觉发现自己处于失去理智的恍惚之前？
在这里想必我们忽略了什么
我们最好放下并且退回线后
有些事人耳听不得
有些事不需要讨论
啊亲爱的，能否别说出去，这事就你知我知？

他们会告诉你这样而告诉我那样
直到我们不知道该信谁
啊亲爱的，能否别说出去，这事就你知我知？

别说出去，这事就你知我知
在事情完全破裂、无法挽回之前
如果我们自己不能搞定
告诉我，我们并不比他们所认为的糟糕
坐在后座指挥的人不知道方向盘的感觉
但是他们当然懂得大惊小怪
啊亲爱的，能否别说出去，这事就你知我知？

能否别说出去，这事就你知我知？

Let's Keep It Between Us

Let's keep it between us
These people meddlin' in our affairs, they're not our friends
Let's keep it between us
Before doors close and our togetherness comes to an end
They'll turn you against me and me against you
'Til we don't know who to trust
Oh, darlin', can we keep it between us?

Let's keep it between us
We've been through too much tough times that they never
    shared
They've had nothing to say to us before
Now all of a sudden it's as if they've always cared
All we need is honesty
A little humility and trust
Oh, darlin', can we keep it between us?

I know we're not perfect
Then again, neither are they
They act like we got to live for them
As if there just ain't no other way
And it's makin' me kind of tired

Can we just lay back for a moment
Before we wake up and find ourselves in a daze that's got us
    out of our minds?
There must be something we're overlooking here
We better drop down now and get back behind the lines
There's some things not fit for human ears

Some things don't need to be discussed
Oh, darlin', can we keep it between us?

They'll tell you one thing and me another
'Til we don't know who to trust
Oh, darlin', can we keep it between us?

Let's keep it between us
Before it all snaps and goes too far
If we can't deal with this by ourselves
Tell me we ain't worse off than they think we are
Backseat drivers don't know the feel of the wheel
But they sure know how to make a fuss
Oh, darlin', can we keep it between us?

Can we keep it between us?

加勒比海的风

她是失乐园的沙仑玫瑰 [1]
来自十字架之地附近的七丘之城 [2]
我在迈阿密上演神曲的戏院演出
她跟我说起耶稣，说起雨
还说起那丛林，她的兄弟们在那儿被害
凶手是一个在大使馆的房顶跳舞的人

她是个孩子还是个女人？我说不清
从一个人到另一个人她切换得轻松
我们进入墙内那里法律的长臂够不着
我是被人当成卒子利用并被捉弄？
这当然有可能，愉快的夜慢慢过去
男人们一边在香水中沐浴，一边赞颂着言论自由

而加勒比海的风还在从拿骚吹到墨西哥
扇着那欲望火炉里的火
而远方的自由船舶在铁浪上是这样英勇不羁

1.《旧约·雅歌》2:1：“我是沙仑的玫瑰花，是谷中的百合花。”
2. 七丘之城，常指罗马，此处可能为耶路撒冷。

令我近处的一切更接近火焰

她的目光穿透衣服看进了我的灵魂
她说："门那边有一个我俩都认识的朋友
你知道吗，他心里总是为我们的最大利益着想"
他交际很广但她的心是个陷阱
她让他死在了那儿
有一些应付账款而他没及时付清

孔雀的叫声，苍蝇在我头上嗡嗡嗡
吊扇坏了，我的床热气腾腾
街头乐队在表演着《更近我主》[1]
我们在教堂尖顶见面那儿回荡着钟声
她说："我知道你在想什么，但其实做什么都
无济于事，我俩就同意我们同意吧"

而加勒比海的风还在从拿骚吹到墨西哥
扇着那欲望火炉里的火
而远方的自由船舶在铁浪上是这样英勇不羁

1.《更近我主》，英国诗人莎拉·亚当斯（Sarah Fuller Flower Adams）创作的赞美诗，后谱成著名小提琴曲。泰坦尼克号沉没前，船上乐队曾演奏此曲，给蒙难者以激励。

令我近处的一切更接近火焰

阴冷、灰暗的大海边的大西洋城
我听到一个声音喊："爸爸。"我总以为是在叫我
但这只是酪乳山的寂静在呼唤
每一个新信使都带来坏消息
关于行军中的军队和所剩无几的时间
关于饥荒和地震和写在墙上的仇恨

我本会娶她吗？我想，我不知道
她在发辫上挂满了铃铛，一直吊向了足尖
但是我一直听见我名字，不得不继续向前
我看见螺丝松了，看见淘气鬼在砸罐头
看见乡下一栋房子从里面被扯烂
听见我的祖先在遥远的国度呼唤

而加勒比海的风还在从拿骚吹到墨西哥
扇着那欲望火炉里的火
而远方的自由船舶在铁浪上是这样英勇不羁
令我近处的一切更接近火焰

Caribbean Wind

She was the rose of Sharon from paradise lost
From the city of seven hills near the place of the cross
I was playing a show in Miami in the theater of divine
    comedy
Told about Jesus, told about the rain
She told me about the jungle where her brothers were slain
By a man who danced on the roof of the embassy

Was she a child or a woman, I can't say which
From one to another she could easily switch
We went into the wall to where the long arm of the law
    could not reach
Could I been used and played as a pawn?
It certainly was possible as the gay night wore on
Where men bathed in perfume and celebrated free speech

And them Caribbean winds still blow from Nassau to
    Mexico
Fanning the flames in the furnace of desire
And them distant ships of liberty on them iron waves so
    bold and free
Bringing everything that's near to me nearer to the fire

She looked into my soul through the clothes that I wore
She said, "We got a mutual friend over by the door
And you know he's got our best interest in mind"
He was well connected but her heart was a snare
And she had left him to die in there
There were payments due and he was a little behind

The cry of the peacock, flies buzz my head
Ceiling fan broken, there's a heat in my bed
Street band playing "Nearer My God to Thee"
We met at the steeple where the mission bells ring
She said, "I know what you're thinking, but there ain't
    a thing
You can do about it, so let us just agree to agree"

And them Caribbean winds still blow from Nassau to
    Mexico
Fanning the flames in the furnace of desire
And them distant ships of liberty on them iron waves so
    bold and free
Bringing everything that's near to me nearer to the fire

Atlantic City by the cold grey sea
I hear a voice crying, "Daddy," I always think it's for me
But it's only the silence in the buttermilk hills that call
Every new messenger brings evil report
'Bout armies on the march and time that is short
And famines and earthquakes and hatred written upon walls

Would I have married her? I don't know, I suppose
She had bells in her braids and they hung to her toes
But I kept hearing my name and had to be movin' on
I saw screws break loose, saw the devil pound tin
I saw a house in the country being torn from within
I heard my ancestors calling from the land far beyond

And them Caribbean winds still blow from Nassau to
    Mexico
Fanning the flames in the furnace of desire

And them distant ships of liberty on them iron waves so
   bold and free
Bringing everything that's near to me nearer to the fire

需要一个女人

沟里终日在下雨，雨水滴进了衣服
我的耐性逐渐失去，鼻子里有团火
我寻找着真理，方式乃上帝设计
真理就是还没找到它，我可能已经被淹死

哦我需要一个女人，是的我要
需要一个女人，是的我要
一个能看懂我的人
一个不在乎的人
而我多想你就是那个女人每一夜
你就是那个女人

我一直在盯着你宝贝，已经差不多五年
你可能压根儿不认识我，但是我见过你的笑和泪水
好啦别吓唬我，我的心在跳
看来有个能给你什么的人，不会对你有啥害处

哦我需要一个女人，啊不是吗
需要一个女人，让家里最终平平安安
看见你转过拐角，看见你靴跟的闪光

看见你在日光中，注视你在黑暗中
而我多想你就是那个女人，好吗
你就是那个女人每夜每夜

哦，假如你信一件事信得够久，你自然就会当真
没有什么墙你跨不过去，没有什么火你穿不过去
哦，信仰是好的，只是别让不好的人知道它的内容
他们会以恶眼看你，用他们的隐藏力量将你驱逐

哦我需要一个女人，让她做我的女王
需要一个女人，明白我意思吧？

Need a Woman

It's been raining in the trenches all day long, dripping down
    to my clothes
My patience is wearing thin, got a fire inside my nose
Searching for the truth the way God designed it
The truth is I might drown before I find it

Well I need a woman, yes I do
Need a woman, yes I do
Someone who can see me as I am
Somebody who just don't give a damn
And I want you to be that woman every night
Be that woman

I've had my eyes on you baby for about five long years
You probably don't know me at all, but I have seen your
    laughter and tears
Now you don't frighten me, my heart is jumping
And you look like it wouldn't hurt you none to have a man
    who could give ya something

Well I need a woman, oh don't I
Need a woman, bring it home safe at last
Seen you turn the corner, seen your boot heels spark
Seen you in the daylight, and watched you in the dark
And I want you to be that woman, all right
Be that woman every night

Well, if you believe in something long enough you just
    naturally come to think it's true

There ain't no wall you can't cross over, ain't no fire you
   can't walk through
Well, believing is all right, just don't let the wrong people
   know what it's all about
They might put the evil eye on you, use their hidden powers
   to try to turn you out

Well I need a woman, just to be my queen
Need a woman, know what I mean?

安吉丽娜

哦，冒险一直是我的本性
右手缩回，而左手伸出去
在一个水流湍急的地方还有猴子跳舞
伴着那六角风琴奏出的调子

我黄头发里的血干了，当我从一个海岸走到另一个海岸
我知道是什么吸引我到你的门前
但不管它是什么吧，它让我觉得你以前见过我
安吉丽娜

啊，安吉丽娜。啊，安吉丽娜

他的眼睛是两道裂缝能让蛇感到骄傲
一张脸画家们都想画当他迈步穿过人群
敬奉一个神，有着大胸女人的身躯
和鬣狗的头

我需要你的允许转过另一边脸吗？[1]

1.《新约·马太福音》5:39，耶稣说："有人打你的右脸，连左边的脸也转过来由他打……"

如果你能读懂我的心，为什么还要我说话？

不，关于那个你要找的人我什么都没听说

安吉丽娜

啊，安吉丽娜。啊，安吉丽娜

巨人谷[1]的星条旗激增

那儿桃子是甜的而奶与蜜四处流

法官派我上路我谨遵着指令

身上带着你的传票

当你停止了存在，那时你会怪谁

我已竭尽全力爱你但我不会玩这个游戏

你最好的朋友和我最坏的敌人是同一个人

安吉丽娜

啊，安吉丽娜。啊，安吉丽娜

---

1. 巨人谷，《旧约·约书亚记》15:8 中，在记载犹大人的领土边界时提到"又上到欣嫩谷西边的山顶，就是在利乏音谷极北的边界"。在英王钦定本中，"利乏音谷"即作"巨人谷"。又，美国作家皮特·B. 凯恩（Peter B. Kyne）于1918 年创作的同名小说，讲述了加利福尼亚的诚恳磨坊主比尔·卡迪根和前来伐木的外来贪婪商人之间的较量，据说迪伦对此部小说颇为欣赏。

一辆黑色梅塞德斯车轮滚过战区

你的仆人们半死不活，你溃烂到了骨头

告诉我，高大的男人们，你们打算到哪儿覆灭

耶路撒冷，还是阿根廷？

在她只有三天大时她被从母亲身边偷走

现在她心满意足报了仇她的财产已经出售

他被上帝的天使包围而她戴着眼罩

你也是这样，安吉丽娜

啊，安吉丽娜。啊，安吉丽娜

我看见一片人海在进军，他们打算用武力占领天堂

我能看见那个不明身份的骑士，我能看见那匹

　　苍白色的马[1]

以上帝的真理告诉我你要什么然后当然你将拥有

来，请下场子吧

沿旋转楼梯而上，开出一条撤退的路

---

1. 苍白色的马，《新约·启示录》19:11："我观看，见天开了。有一匹白马，骑在马上的称为诚信真实，他审判、争战都按着公义。"

经过冒烟的树，经过那四脸天使 [1]

乞求上帝怜悯，并且在不洁之地哭泣

安吉丽娜

啊，安吉丽娜。啊，安吉丽娜

---

1. 四脸天使，《旧约·以西结书》1:6-10，以西结所见异象中，有四张脸孔的活物，四张脸孔分别是人脸、狮子脸、牛脸和鹰脸。又，《以西结书》10:14："基路伯各有四脸：第一是基路伯的脸，第二是人的脸，第三是狮子的脸，第四是鹰的脸。"

Angelina

Well, it's always been my nature to take chances
My right hand drawing back while my left hand advances
Where the current is strong and the monkey dances
To the tune of a concertina

Blood dryin' in my yellow hair as I go from shore to shore
I know what it is that has drawn me to your door
But whatever it could be, makes me think you've seen me
  before
Angelina

Oh, Angelina. Oh, Angelina

His eyes were two slits that would make a snake proud
With a face that any painter would paint as he walked
  through the crowd
Worshipping a god with the body of a woman well endowed
And the head of a hyena

Do I need your permission to turn the other cheek?
If you can read my mind, why must I speak?
No, I have heard nothing about the man that you seek
Angelina

Oh, Angelina. Oh, Angelina

In the valley of the giants where the stars and stripes explode
The peaches they were sweet and the milk and honey flowed

I was only following instructions when the judge sent me
  down the road
With your subpoena

When you cease to exist, then who will you blame
I've tried my best to love you but I cannot play this game
Your best friend and my worst enemy is one and the same
Angelina

Oh, Angelina. Oh, Angelina

There's a black Mercedes rollin' through the combat zone
Your servants are half dead, you're down to the bone
Tell me, tall men, where would you like to be overthrown
Maybe down in Jerusalem or Argentina?

She was stolen from her mother when she was three days old
Now her vengeance has been satisfied and her possessions
  have been sold
He's surrounded by God's angels and she's wearin'
  a blindfold
And so are you, Angelina

Oh, Angelina. Oh, Angelina

I see pieces of men marching, trying to take heaven by force
I can see the unknown rider, I can see the pale white horse
In God's truth tell me what you want and you'll have it
  of course
Just step into the arena

Beat a path of retreat up them spiral staircases
Pass the tree of smoke, pass the angel with four faces

Begging God for mercy and weepin' in unholy places
Angelina

Oh, Angelina. Oh, Angelina

你改变了我的生活

我在听死亡游行的声音
它唱着阴谋，想让我恐惧
为我不能理解和相信的系统工作
受奚落折磨，渴望在厌恶中彻底放弃

但是你改变了我的生活
在冲突四起的时候不期而至
怀着饥渴和需要，你让我的心流血
你改变了我的生活

谈论着拯救，人们突然厌倦
他们有一百万件事要做，他们全都欢欣鼓舞
你在行魔鬼的作为，你有一百万个朋友
当你有了收获他们全在那儿，最后他们会把它全拿走

但是你改变了我的生活
在冲突四起的时候不期而至
我被枪指着，乌云挡住了太阳
你改变了我的生活

哦，人的本性就是乞和偷
我自己干，它不是那么不真实
野性的呼唤永远在拍打我的门
想让我像雄鹰翱翔而我其实是被铐在地上

但是你改变了我的生活
在冲突四起的时候不期而至
从银和金到人无法控制的
你改变了我的生活

我和猪一起从花式盘里吃饭
人们告诉我我看着很好，并祝我度过美好的一天
一切似乎很得体，一切似乎很高档
吃着那绝对的垃圾举止如此矜持

但是你改变了我的生活
在冲突四起的时候不期而至
从银和金到人无法控制的
你改变了我的生活

你在阳光中容光焕发同时也是如此平静宁和
而人类的孤儿应着棕榈的节拍在跳舞

你的眼目如火焰，你的脚是铜做的 [1]
在你创造的世界中，他们抛弃了你 [2]

你改变了我的生活
在冲突四起的时候不期而至
从银和金到人无法控制的
你改变了我的生活

在我身体里有个我几乎看不见的人
侵入我的隐私，帮我做决定
拉住我，不让我站起来
让我感到自己像在外邦作了寄居的

但是你改变了我的生活
在冲突四起的时候不期而至
你出现了，给我一个新心灵
你改变了我的生活

我主与救主，我的伴侣，我的朋友

1.《新约·启示录》2:18，耶稣形容自己是"那眼目如火焰，脚像光明铜的神之子"。
2.《新约·约翰福音》1:10："他在世界，世界也是藉着他造的，世界却不认识他。"

他又是修复心灵的人，监管意志的人，最终的真实
我的造物主，我的慰藉者，我快乐的根由
那个世界所反对却永不能摧毁的

你改变了我的生活
在冲突四起的时候不期而至
你像风一样进来了，像埃罗尔·弗林[1]
你改变了我的生活

---

1. 埃罗尔·弗林（Errol Flynn，1909—1959），美国演员，以饰演侠盗著
称，主演过《罗宾汉历险记》（The Adventures of Robin Hood，1938）等，
一生放纵不羁、爱酒好色，有名言："我爱威士忌年久、女人年轻。"

You Changed My Life

I was listening to the voices of death on parade
Singing about conspiracy, wanted me to be afraid
Working for a system I couldn't understand or trust
Suffered ridicule and wanting to give it all up in disgust

But you changed my life
Came along in a time of strife
In hunger and need, you made my heart bleed
You changed my life

Talk about salvation, people suddenly get tired
They got a million things to do, they're all so inspired
You do the work of the devil, you got a million friends
They'll be there when you got something, they'll take it all
    in the end

But you changed my life
Came along in a time of strife
I was under the gun, clouds blocking the sun
You changed my life

Well, the nature of man is to beg and to steal
I do it myself, it's not so unreal
The call of the wild is forever at my door
Wants me to fly like an eagle while being chained to the
    floor

But you changed my life
Came along in a time of strife

From silver and gold to what man cannot hold
You changed my life

I was eating with the pigs off a fancy tray
I was told I was looking good and to have a nice day
It all seemed so proper, it all seemed so elite
Eating that absolute garbage while being so discreet

But you changed my life
Came along in a time of strife
From silver and gold to what man cannot hold
You changed my life

You were glowing in the sun while being peaceably calm
While orphans of man danced to the beat of the palm
Your eyes were on fire, your feet were of brass
In the world you had made they made you an outcast

You changed my life
Came along in a time of strife
From silver and gold to what man cannot hold
You changed my life

There was someone in my body that I could hardly see
Invading my privacy making my decisions for me
Holding me back, not letting me stand
Making me feel like a stranger in a strange land

But you changed my life
Came along in a time of strife
You come down the line, gave me a new mind
You changed my life

My Lord and my Savior, my companion, my friend
Heart fixer, mind regulator, true to the end
My creator, my comforter, my cause for joy
What the world is set against but will never destroy

You changed my life
Came along in a time of strife
You came in like the wind, like Errol Flynn
You changed my life

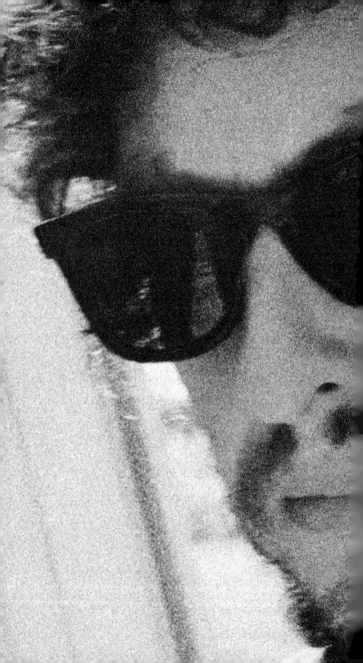

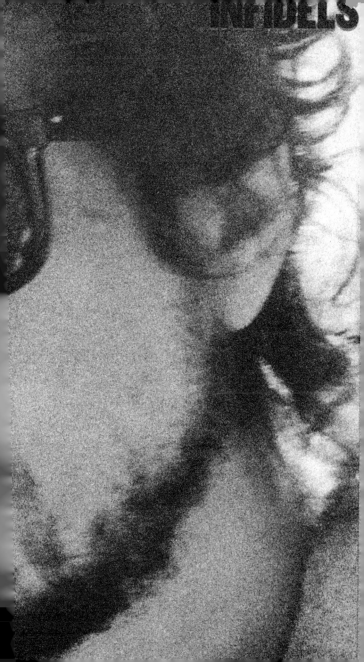

They say that oppression is a cruel tutor YOU KNOW NEWS OF YOU HAS COM
And injustice is a nurse DOWN THE LINE EVEN BEFORE YA CAME IN THE DOOR
You can put your hand in the hand of a man with a nose that can't smell THEY SA
But you put your confidence in him and that's worse IN YOUR FATHER'S HOUSE
Snap out of it, baby THERE'S MANY MANSIONS — EACH ONE OF 'M GOT A
People are jealous of you
They smile in your face, but behind your back they hiss FIRE PROOF FLOOR
What's a sweetheart like you doin' in a dump like this

异教徒
Infidels

陈震 译

 1983 年 10 月，鲍勃·迪伦发表了他的第二十二张录音室专辑《异教徒》。录音乐手阵容简洁有力：恐怖海峡乐队的马克·诺弗勒（Mark Knopfler）和艾伦·克拉克（Alan Clark），前滚石乐队的米克·泰勒（Mick Taylor），来自牙买加的斯莱·邓巴（Sly Dunbar）和罗比·莎士比亚（Robbie Shakespeare），加上迪伦。担纲制作的是马克·诺弗勒和迪伦自己。

 20 世纪 70 年代末，迪伦皈依基督教，在 1979 年至 1981 年连发三张福音专辑，即所谓的"基督教三部曲"。到了 1982 年，他的宗教狂热开始退潮，与宗教无关的旧作悄悄回到了他的演出曲目中，酒精、咖啡因和性躁动也重新走进了他的生活。《异教徒》创作于这一阶段，是他拥抱世俗音乐的一张回归之作。专辑里除了有"爱情"和"失去"这样的私人主题，还有他对环境和地缘政治的思考。不过，迪伦并未放弃他的信仰，许多宗教意象被他巧妙地融进了歌词。在《滚石》杂志的克里斯托弗·康奈利（Christopher Connelly）等乐评人看来，《异教徒》让迪伦的音乐事业又焕发了生机，是继《轨道上的血》后的又一张经典。除了创作和演唱备受评论界好评，这张专辑也取得了商业上的成功。

陈震

小丑

站在水面抛撒面包 [1]

铁头神像眼神闪耀

远船驶进薄雾

飓风呼啸，你双手各攥一蛇降临世间

自由近在眼前

但若真理远在天边，自由又有何用？

小丑随着夜莺的歌声翩翩起舞

鸟儿借着月亮的光辉展翅高飞

哦，哦，哦，小丑

太阳飞快西沉

你起身，跟空无一人说再见

傻瓜们冲进的地方，天使不敢涉足

他们的未来，都充满恐惧，你毫不表露

再脱掉一层皮肤

比里面的迫害者领先一步

1.《旧约·传道书》11:1："当将你的粮食撒在水面，因为日久必能得着。"另，
"站在水面"亦见《新约·马太福音》14:22-33。

小丑随着夜莺的歌声翩翩起舞

鸟儿借着月亮的光辉展翅高飞

哦，哦，哦，小丑

你是大山的男人，能漫步云端

操控百姓，扭曲梦境

你将去所多玛和蛾摩拉[1]

但与你何干？那里无人愿娶你的妹妹[2]

殉道者的朋友，风流妇的朋友

你窥视烈火的熔炉，看到无名的财主[3]

小丑随着夜莺的歌声翩翩起舞

鸟儿借着月亮的光辉展翅高飞

哦，哦，哦，小丑

嗯，《利未记》和《申命记》

丛林和海洋法则是你唯一的老师

---

1. 所多玛和蛾摩拉，两座被上帝毁灭的罪恶之城。
2.《旧约·创世记》12:20–20:15，亚伯拉罕之妹撒拉先后为埃及法老王与基拉耳王亚比米勒所娶，但上帝插手干预，制止两王侵犯她。两王皆把撒拉归还亚伯拉罕。
3.《新约·路加福音》16:19–31，财主在烈火中受苦。

薄暮之烟里，你驾着乳白色的骏骑 [1]
米开朗基罗差点就雕出了你的五官
你在田间歇息，远离动荡之地
在繁星旁半眠，小狗舔你的脸

小丑随着夜莺的歌声翩翩起舞
鸟儿借着月亮的光辉展翅高飞
哦，哦，哦，小丑

嗯，步枪手在潜近病残
传教士亦在尾随，谁先到达无法确定
警棍、水炮、催泪弹、挂锁
燃烧弹和石头，在每一张幕布背后
背信弃义的审判官在自己织的罗网里残喘
黑夜降临只是时间早晚

小丑随着夜莺的歌声翩翩起舞
鸟儿借着月亮的光辉展翅高飞
哦，哦，哦，小丑

1.《新约·启示录》19:11："我观看，见天开了。有一匹白马，骑在马上的称
为诚信真实，他审判、争战都按着公义。"

幽暗的世界，易变的灰天

女人今天刚诞下王子，给他穿上一身猩红

他将把牧师装进口袋，把刀刃加热

从街头带走没妈的孩子，放到一个娼妓脚边

哦，小丑，他的所求你心知肚明

哦，小丑，你没作任何回应

小丑随着夜莺的歌声翩翩起舞

鸟儿借着月亮的光辉展翅高飞

哦，哦，哦，小丑

Jokerman

Standing on the waters casting your bread
While the eyes of the idol with the iron head are glowing
Distant ships sailing into the mist
You were born with a snake in both of your fists while a
    hurricane was blowing
Freedom just around the corner for you
But with the truth so far off, what good will it do?

Jokerman dance to the nightingale tune
Bird fly high by the light of the moon
Oh, oh, oh, Jokerman

So swiftly the sun sets in the sky
You rise up and say goodbye to no one
Fools rush in where angels fear to tread
Both of their futures, so full of dread, you don't show one
Shedding off one more layer of skin
Keeping one step ahead of the persecutor within

Jokerman dance to the nightingale tune
Bird fly high by the light of the moon
Oh, oh, oh, Jokerman

You're a man of the mountains, you can walk on the clouds
Manipulator of crowds, you're a dream twister
You're going to Sodom and Gomorrah
But what do you care? Ain't nobody there would want to
    marry your sister
Friend to the martyr, a friend to the woman of shame

You look into the fiery furnace, see the rich man without any name

Jokerman dance to the nightingale tune
Bird fly high by the light of the moon
Oh, oh, oh, Jokerman

Well, the Book of Leviticus and Deuteronomy
The law of the jungle and the sea are your only teachers
In the smoke of the twilight on a milk-white steed
Michelangelo indeed could've carved out your features
Resting in the fields, far from the turbulent space
Half asleep near the stars with a small dog licking your face

Jokerman dance to the nightingale tune
Bird fly high by the light of the moon
Oh, oh, oh, Jokerman

Well, the rifleman's stalking the sick and the lame
Preacherman seeks the same, who'll get there first is uncertain
Nightsticks and water cannons, tear gas, padlocks
Molotov cocktails and rocks behind every curtain
False-hearted judges dying in the webs that they spin
Only a matter of time 'til night comes steppin' in

Jokerman dance to the nightingale tune
Bird fly high by the light of the moon
Oh, oh, oh, Jokerman

It's a shadowy world, skies are slippery grey
A woman just gave birth to a prince today and dressed him in scarlet

He'll put the priest in his pocket, put the blade to the heat
Take the motherless children off the street and place them
    at the feet of a harlot
Oh, Jokerman, you know what he wants
Oh, Jokerman, you don't show any response

Jokerman dance to the nightingale tune
Bird fly high by the light of the moon
Oh, oh, oh, Jokerman

像你这样的甜心

哦，压力小了，老板不在
他去了北方，不在身旁
他们说他已被虚荣征服
但他确实在日落后离去
顺便说一下，那是一顶可爱的帽子
那微笑如此难以抗拒
但像你这样的甜心，在这脏地方干吗？

你知道吗，我曾经认识一个长得像你的女人
她想要一个完整的男人，而不只是一半
当我还是个孩子时，她叫我甜心老爸
你笑的时候，让我想起了她
为了在这局牌中发牌，得让皇后消失
手腕一抖就已搞定
像你这样的甜心，在这脏地方干吗？

你知道吗，你这样的女人应该待在家
那是属于你的地方
留心一个真正爱你的人
一个会永远对你好的人

你能忍受多少打骂？

初吻时你无从料到

像你这样的甜心，在这脏地方干吗？

你知道你能闯出名气

你能听到他们的轮胎尖叫

爬过雕花玻璃来交易的女人里

没人比你更美丽

你知道吗，关于你的消息已经浮现

甚至在你进门之前

他们说，你父亲的家里有许多住处 [1]

每处都铺着防火地板

打起精神来，宝贝儿，人们嫉妒你

他们对着你的脸微笑，对着你的背嘲笑

像你这样的甜心，在这脏地方干吗？

在这里得成为一个重要的人，亲爱的

得干一些邪恶的事情

得有自己的后宫，当你进了门

1.《新约·约翰福音》14:2："在我父的家里有许多住处；若是没有，我就早已告诉你们了。我去原是为你们预备地方去。"

得吹你的口琴，吹到嘴唇出血

他们说爱国主义是最后的庇护所

一个无赖紧紧抓住了它

偷得少他们送你进监牢

偷得多他们让你当皇帝

这里只有一步之遥，宝贝儿

它叫永恒极乐之地

像你这样的甜心，在这脏地方干吗？

Sweetheart Like You

Well, the pressure's down, the boss ain't here
He gone North, he ain't around
They say that vanity got the best of him
But he sure left here after sundown
By the way, that's a cute hat
And that smile's so hard to resist
But what's a sweetheart like you doin' in a dump like this?

You know, I once knew a woman who looked like you
She wanted a whole man, not just a half
She used to call me sweet daddy when I was only a child
You kind of remind me of her when you laugh
In order to deal in this game, got to make the queen
    disappear
It's done with a flick of the wrist
What's a sweetheart like you doin' in a dump like this?

You know, a woman like you should be at home
That's where you belong
Watching out for someone who loves you true
Who would never do you wrong
Just how much abuse will you be able to take?
Well, there's no way to tell by that first kiss
What's a sweetheart like you doin' in a dump like this?

You know you can make a name for yourself
You can hear them tires squeal
You can be known as the most beautiful woman
Who ever crawled across cut glass to make a deal

You know, news of you has come down the line
Even before ya came in the door
They say in your father's house, there's many mansions
Each one of them got a fireproof floor
Snap out of it, baby, people are jealous of you
They smile to your face, but behind your back they hiss
What's a sweetheart like you doin' in a dump like this?

Got to be an important person to be in here, honey
Got to have done some evil deed
Got to have your own harem when you come in the door
Got to play your harp until your lips bleed

They say that patriotism is the last refuge
To which a scoundrel clings
Steal a little and they throw you in jail
Steal a lot and they make you king
There's only one step down from here, baby
It's called the land of permanent bliss
What's a sweetheart like you doin' in a dump like this?

街坊恶霸

哦，街坊恶霸，他只是一个男人
他的敌人说他占了他们的土地
他们的人数是他的一百万倍 [1]
他无处可逃，无路可跑
他是街坊恶霸

街坊恶霸只是为了活下去
他因活着受到批评和谴责
他不应该还手，他应该脸皮厚
他应该躺下来受死，当他的门被踢开
他是街坊恶霸

街坊恶霸被逐出每一片土地
他在地球上游荡，一个被放逐的人
他的家人流落四方，他的人民饱受侵扰
他永远因为降生而受审

---

1. 在 1967 年 6 月的第三次中东战争里，以色列六天内击败了埃及、约旦、
叙利亚联军，占领了埃及的西奈半岛、叙利亚的戈兰高地、加沙地带、约旦河
西岸和耶路撒冷旧城。

他是街坊恶霸

哦，他击昏一个动私刑的暴民，他受到了批评
老太太谴责他，说他应该道歉
然后他摧毁了一个炸弹工厂，没有人高兴
这些炸弹是为他准备的，他应该感到难过 [1]
他是街坊恶霸

哦，他会遵守世界为他制定的规则？
机会不大，概率太低
因为他的脖上套着绞索，后背顶着把枪
杀他的执照颁发给了每个杀人狂
他是街坊恶霸

他没有真正的盟友
他想得到什么必须付钱，没人出于爱送给他
他买废旧武器时不会被拒绝
但没人送来血肉之躯与他并肩拼杀
他是街坊恶霸

---

1. 指 1981 年以色列对伊拉克奥斯拉克核反应堆的摧毁，或之前对阿拉伯国家军工厂的轰炸。

哦，他周围的人都是和平主义者
他们每晚祈祷杀戮结束
他们连一只苍蝇都不忍伤害，伤害一只他们会流泪
他们躺着，等着街坊恶霸入睡
他是街坊恶霸

每个奴役过他的帝国都不复存在
埃及和罗马，甚至伟大的巴比伦
他在沙漠中造了一个天堂花园
不与谁结党，不受谁管辖
他是街坊恶霸

如今他最神圣的书被人践踏
他签的所有条约都是不平等条约
他拿走世界的饼屑，把它变成财富
拿走世界的疾病，把它变成健康
他是街坊恶霸

你们感激他做了哪些事？
不感激，他们说。他只是喜欢引发战争
的确是傲慢、偏见与迷信
他们等待街坊恶霸，像狗等待喂食
他是街坊恶霸

他做了什么，怎么一身伤疤？

他改变了河水的流向吗？污染了月亮和星星吗？

街坊恶霸，站在山巅

拖延时间，时间凝固

街坊恶霸

Neighborhood Bully

Well, the neighborhood bully, he's just one man
His enemies say he's on their land
They got him outnumbered about a million to one
He got no place to escape to, no place to run
He's the neighborhood bully

The neighborhood bully just lives to survive
He's criticized and condemned for being alive
He's not supposed to fight back, he's supposed to have thick
  skin
He's supposed to lay down and die when his door is kicked
  in
He's the neighborhood bully

The neighborhood bully been driven out of every land
He's wandered the earth an exiled man
Seen his family scattered, his people hounded and torn
He's always on trial for just being born
He's the neighborhood bully

Well, he knocked out a lynch mob, he was criticized
Old women condemned him, said he should apologize
Then he destroyed a bomb factory, nobody was glad
The bombs were meant for him. He was supposed to feel
  bad
He's the neighborhood bully

Well, the chances are against it and the odds are slim
That he'll live by the rules that the world makes for him

'Cause there's a noose at his neck and a gun at his back
And a license to kill him is given out to every maniac
He's the neighborhood bully

He got no allies to really speak of
What he gets he must pay for, he don't get it out of love
He buys obsolete weapons and he won't be denied
But no one sends flesh and blood to fight by his side
He's the neighborhood bully

Well, he's surrounded by pacifists who all want peace
They pray for it nightly that the bloodshed must cease
Now, they wouldn't hurt a fly. To hurt one they would
    weep
They lay and they wait for this bully to fall asleep
He's the neighborhood bully

Every empire that's enslaved him is gone
Egypt and Rome, even the great Babylon
He's made a garden of paradise in the desert sand
In bed with nobody, under no one's command
He's the neighborhood bully

Now his holiest books have been trampled upon
No contract he signed was worth what it was written on
He took the crumbs of the world and he turned it into
    wealth
Took sickness and disease and he turned it into health
He's the neighborhood bully

What's anybody indebted to him for?
Nothin', they say. He just likes to cause war
Pride and prejudice and superstition indeed

They wait for this bully like a dog waits to feed
He's the neighborhood bully

What has he done to wear so many scars?
Does he change the course of rivers? Does he pollute the
    moon and stars?
Neighborhood bully, standing on the hill
Running out the clock, time standing still
Neighborhood bully

杀人执照

他认为，他是地球的统治者，所以可以为所欲为
如果事情没有马上改变，他会
噢，他一手导演了自己的劫数
第一步是触摸月球 [1]

现在，有个女人在我的街区
她就坐在那，长夜渐静
她说谁来吊销他的杀人执照？

现在，他们带走他，教化他，训练他
把他引向毁灭之路
然后在他身上盖上星条旗
像卖二手车一样卖掉他的尸体

现在，有个女人在我的街区
她就坐在那，面对着山丘
她说谁来吊销他的杀人执照？

---

1. 指涉美国的太空计划。

现在，他决意毁灭，他害怕又困扰

他已被高超地洗脑

他只相信自己的眼睛

而他的眼睛，只是在对他说谎

但有个女人在我的街区

坐在那瑟瑟发抖

她说谁来吊销他的杀人执照？

你可能是噪音制造者、灵魂制造者

负心者、勤劳者

全力以赴

也可能是阴谋里的一颗棋子

那是你得到的一切

直到你幡然醒悟

现在，他在一坛死水的祭坛上自我崇拜

他看到自己的倒影，心满意足

噢，他反对公平竞争

他什么都想要，还得以他的方式

现在，有个女人在我的街区

她就坐在那，长夜渐静

她说谁来吊销他的杀人执照？

License to Kill

Man thinks 'cause he rules the earth he can do with it as he
  please
And if things don't change soon, he will
Oh, man has invented his doom
First step was touching the moon

Now, there's a woman on my block
She just sit there as the night grows still
She say who gonna take away his license to kill?

Now, they take him and they teach him and they groom
  him for life
And they set him on a path where he's bound to get ill
Then they bury him with stars
Sell his body like they do used cars

Now, there's a woman on my block
She just sit there facin' the hill
She say who gonna take away his license to kill?

Now, he's hell-bent for destruction, he's afraid and confused
And his brain has been mismanaged with great skill
All he believes are his eyes
And his eyes, they just tell him lies

But there's a woman on my block
Sitting there in a cold chill
She say who gonna take away his license to kill?

Ya may be a noisemaker, spirit maker
Heartbreaker, backbreaker
Leave no stone unturned
May be an actor in a plot
That might be all that you got
'Til your error you clearly learn

Now he worships at an altar of a stagnant pool
And when he sees his reflection, he's fulfilled
Oh, man is opposed to fair play
He wants it all and he wants it his way

Now, there's a woman on my block
She just sit there as the night grows still
She say who gonna take away his license to kill?

和平使者

朝窗外看，宝贝儿，有你想捕捉的镜头

乐队在演奏《迪克西》[1]，一个男人伸出他的手

可能是纳粹元首[2]

可能是当地牧师

你知道撒旦会扮成和平使者

他伶牙俐齿，声音动人

知道人类唱过的每一首情歌

好意会坏事

双手会沾满油脂

你知道撒旦会扮成和平使者

嗯，他先是在幕后，然后到台前

双眼看起来像在猎兔

1.《迪克西》，19 世纪最著名的美国歌曲之一，一般认为作者是美国词曲作家丹·埃米特（Dan Emmett）。原曲描写了一位黑人对南方故土的乡愁，后经改编成为美国南北战争时期流行于南方蓄奴州邦联的战歌，并逐步演化为美国南方的标志。随着 20 世纪 50 年代美国黑人民权运动兴起，此歌被认为带有强烈的种族主义色彩。

2. 原文为德语。

没人能识破他

没人能，连警察局长都不能

你知道撒旦会扮成和平使者

嗯，他抓住你，当你希望瞥见太阳

抓住你，当你深陷麻烦之中

他可能就站在你旁边

看着最不起眼

我听说撒旦会扮成和平使者

嗯，他可能迷人，也可能迟钝

他能坐进用你的头骨做的桶，顺着尼亚加拉大瀑布漂流
　　而下

我闻到了做菜的味道

我敢说那是一顿大餐

你知道撒旦会扮成和平使者

他是伟大的人道主义者，他是伟大的慈善家

他知道你哪里敏感，亲爱的，还有你想怎么接吻

他会用双臂搂着你

你能感受到野兽的温柔触碰

你知道撒旦会扮成和平使者

嗯，今晚嚎狼会嚎叫，王蛇会爬行

矗立千年的树会突然跌倒

想结婚吗？现在就结

明天一切活动都将终了

你知道撒旦会扮成和平使者

妈妈在为她的蓝眼睛男孩哭泣

她抱着小白鞋和那个小破玩具

他追随一颗星星而去

那三人从东方一路追随的那一颗[1]

我听说撒旦会扮成和平使者

1.《新约·马太福音》2:1-11，东方三位博士见伯利恒上空有一颗星，于是随之行至耶稣的出生地。

Man of Peace

Look out your window, baby, there's a scene you'd like to
    catch
The band is playing "Dixie," a man got his hand outstretched
Could be the Führer
Could be the local priest
You know sometimes Satan comes as a man of peace

He got a sweet gift of gab, he got a harmonious tongue
He knows every song of love that ever has been sung
Good intentions can be evil
Both hands can be full of grease
You know that sometimes Satan comes as a man of peace

Well, first he's in the background, then he's in the front
Both eyes are looking like they're on a rabbit hunt
Nobody can see through him
No, not even the Chief of Police
You know that sometimes Satan comes as a man of peace

Well, he catch you when you're hoping for a glimpse of the
    sun
Catch you when your troubles feel like they weigh a ton
He could be standing next to you
The person that you'd notice least
I hear that sometimes Satan comes as a man of peace

Well, he can be fascinating, he can be dull
He can ride down Niagara Falls in the barrels of your skull
I can smell something cooking

I can tell there's going to be a feast
You know that sometimes Satan comes as a man of peace

He's a great humanitarian, he's a great philanthropist
He knows just where to touch you, honey, and how you like
   to be kissed
He'll put both his arms around you
You can feel the tender touch of the beast
You know that sometimes Satan comes as a man of peace

Well, the howling wolf will howl tonight, the king snake
   will crawl
Trees that've stood for a thousand years suddenly will fall
Wanna get married? Do it now
Tomorrow all activity will cease
You know that sometimes Satan comes as a man of peace

Somewhere Mama's weeping for her blue-eyed boy
She's holding them little white shoes and that little broken
   toy
And he's following a star
The same one them three men followed from the East
I hear that sometimes Satan comes as a man of peace

工会日落西山

哦，我的鞋来自新加坡

我的手电筒来自台湾

我的桌布来自马来西亚

我的皮带扣来自亚马逊

你知道吗，我穿的这件衬衫来自菲律宾

我开的车是一辆雪佛兰

它在阿根廷组装

把它组装好的家伙一天挣三毛

哦，工会日落西山

还有美国制造

这主意真好

直到贪婪挡道

哦，丝绸晚礼服来自香港

珍珠来自日本

狗项圈来自印度

花盆来自巴基斯坦

所有的家具，上面写着"巴西制造"

那里有个女人，肯定拼命苦干

一天给一家十二口带回三毛

你知道吗，那对她来说是笔巨款

哦，工会日落西山

还有美国制造

这主意真好

直到贪婪挡道

嗯，你知道吗，许多人抱怨没有工作

我说："为什么这么说

当你买到的没有一样是美国货？"

他们什么都不在美国造了

你知道吗，资本主义高于法律

它说："卖出去才算数"

当在国内造成本太高

你就会到更便宜的地方造

哦，工会日落西山

还有美国制造

这主意真好

直到贪婪挡道

哦，你曾经拥有的工作

被他们送去了萨尔瓦多

工会是大组织，朋友

他们像恐龙一样外出

他们过去在堪萨斯种粮食

现在想在月球上种并生吃

我看到那一天即将来到，当你自家的花园

都将违反法律

哦，工会日落西山

还有美国制造

这主意真好

直到贪婪挡道

民主不统治世界

你最好明白这件事

这个世界由暴力统治

但我想还是不说出来更好

从百老汇到银河

确实是巨大的版图

一个男人别无选择

当他饥肠辘辘

哦，工会日落西山

还有美国制造

这主意真好

直到贪婪挡道

Union Sundown

Well, my shoes, they come from Singapore
My flashlight's from Taiwan
My tablecloth's from Malaysia
My belt buckle's from the Amazon
You know, this shirt I wear comes from the Philippines
And the car I drive is a Chevrolet
It was put together down in Argentina
By a guy makin' thirty cents a day

Well, it's sundown on the union
And what's made in the U.S.A.
Sure was a good idea
'Til greed got in the way

Well, this silk dress is from Hong Kong
And the pearls are from Japan
Well, the dog collar's from India
And the flower pot's from Pakistan
All the furniture, it says "Made in Brazil"
Where a woman, she slaved for sure
Bringin' home thirty cents a day to a family of twelve
You know, that's a lot of money to her

Well, it's sundown on the union
And what's made in the U.S.A.
Sure was a good idea
'Til greed got in the way

Well, you know, lots of people complainin' that there is no work

I say, "Why you say that for
When nothin' you got is U.S.–made?"
They don't make nothin' here no more
You know, capitalism is above the law
It say, "It don't count 'less it sells"
When it costs too much to build it at home
You just build it cheaper someplace else

Well, it's sundown on the union
And what's made in the U.S.A.
Sure was a good idea
'Til greed got in the way

Well, the job that you used to have
They gave it to somebody down in El Salvador
The unions are big business, friend
And they're goin' out like a dinosaur
They used to grow food in Kansas
Now they want to grow it on the moon and eat it raw
I can see the day coming when even your home garden
Is gonna be against the law

Well, it's sundown on the union
And what's made in the U.S.A.
Sure was a good idea
'Til greed got in the way

Democracy don't rule the world
You'd better get that in your head
This world is ruled by violence
But I guess that's better left unsaid
From Broadway to the Milky Way
That's a lot of territory indeed

And a man's gonna do what he has to do
When he's got a hungry mouth to feed

Well, it's sundown on the union
And what's made in the U.S.A.
Sure was a good idea
'Til greed got in the way

我和我

已经太久没有陌生女人睡在我床上
看她睡得多香,她的梦一定自由欢畅
来世她定能拥有世界,或忠诚地嫁给
月下溪旁,撰写圣诗的正义国王

我和我
我生来不高尚也不能原谅对方
我和我
一个对另一个说,睹我容颜者皆亡 [1]

我想出去散步
这儿没发生什么,什么也没发生
此外,如果她现在醒来,她只想听我讲
但我无话可讲,什么都不想说

我和我
我生来不高尚也不能原谅对方

1.《旧约·出埃及记》33:20,耶和华对摩西说:"你们不能看见我的面,因为
人见我的面不能存活。"

我和我

一个对另一个说，睹我容颜者皆亡

走过一回人迹罕至的小路，跑得快的不会赢得比赛 [1]

胜利属于能分解真理的道者 [2]

需要一个陌生人来教导我，让我看清正义美丽的脸庞

让我看明以眼还眼，以牙还牙

我和我

我生来不高尚也不能原谅对方

我和我

一个对另一个说，睹我容颜者皆亡

除了火车月台上的两个人，谁都看不见

他们等待着春天，沿着铁轨抽着烟

今晚世界会灭亡，但这没关系

她应该还在安睡，当我回到那里

我和我

1.《旧约·传道书》9:11："快跑的未必能赢。"

2.《新约·提摩太后书》2:15："你当竭力在神面前得蒙喜悦，作无愧的工人，按着正意分解真理的道。"

我生来不高尚也不能原谅对方

我和我

一个对另一个说，睹我容颜者皆亡

正午，我仍逼着自己走在这条路上，最黑暗的一段

进入狭窄的小巷，我不能绊倒或原地踏步

有人用我的嘴说话，但我只听自己的心

我给大家都做了鞋子，甚至包括你，而我依然赤脚走路

我和我

我生来不高尚也不能原谅对方

我和我

一个对另一个说，睹我容颜者皆亡

I and I

Been so long since a strange woman has slept in my bed
Look how sweet she sleeps, how free must be her dreams
In another lifetime she must have owned the world, or been
    faithfully wed
To some righteous king who wrote psalms beside moonlit
    streams

I and I
In creation where one's nature neither honors nor forgives
I and I
One says to the other, no man sees my face and lives

Think I'll go out and go for a walk
Not much happenin' here, nothin' ever does
Besides, if she wakes up now, she'll just want me to talk
I got nothin' to say, 'specially about whatever was

I and I
In creation where one's nature neither honors nor forgives
I and I
One says to the other, no man sees my face and lives

Took an untrodden path once, where the swift don't win
    the race
It goes to the worthy, who can divide the word of truth
Took a stranger to teach me, to look into justice's beautiful
    face
And to see an eye for an eye and a tooth for a tooth

I and I
In creation where one's nature neither honors nor forgives
I and I
One says to the other, no man sees my face and lives

Outside of two men on a train platform there's nobody
    in sight
They're waiting for spring to come, smoking down the track
The world could come to an end tonight, but that's all right
She should still be there sleepin' when I get back

I and I
In creation where one's nature neither honors nor forgives
I and I
One says to the other, no man sees my face and lives

Noontime, and I'm still pushin' myself along the road, the
    darkest part
Into the narrow lanes, I can't stumble or stay put
Someone else is speakin' with my mouth, but I'm listening
    only to my heart
I've made shoes for everyone, even you, while I still
    go barefoot

I and I
In creation where one's nature neither honors nor forgives
I and I
One says to the other, no man sees my face and lives

今晚坚强些，别崩溃

等一下再走，女孩
等一下再去拉门
你想达成什么，女孩？
我们可以再谈一谈？
你知道吗，街上到处都是毒蛇
它们丧失了所有希望
你知道，就连教皇的宫殿里
都不再安全 [1]

今晚坚强些，别崩溃
我怕是没法应对
今晚坚强些，别崩溃
昨天不过是回忆
明天永远事与愿违
我需要你，对

从那边过来，女孩

---

1. 1981 年 5 月 13 日，罗马天主教第 264 任教宗若望·保禄二世在梵蒂冈圣伯多禄广场准备演讲时遭到枪击。

坐在这里。你可以坐我的座位
我看不到我们有未来，女孩
唯一开着的地方在千里之外，我不能带你去
我希望我是医生
也许能挽回几条失去的人命
也许能在这世界上做些好事
而不是烧掉走过的每一座桥

今晚坚强些，别崩溃
我怕是没法应对
今晚坚强些，别崩溃
昨天不过是回忆
明天永远事与愿违
我需要你，对

我不太善于交谈，女孩
所以你可能不了解我的感受
但是如果我可以，我会带你到山顶，女孩
给你建一座不锈钢的房屋
但我就像被困在一幅
挂在卢浮宫里的画中
我的喉咙和鼻子开始发痒
但我知道自己无法动弹

今晚坚强些，别崩溃

我怕是没法应对

今晚坚强些，别崩溃

昨天已逝，但往昔永存

明天不过一步之遥

而我需要你，对

那些朝你走来的是什么人？

你认识他们？会打一架？

他们缺乏幽默感的微笑那么容易被看穿

他们能告诉你孰是孰非？

你还记得圣詹姆斯街？

在那里你让杰姬·P. 兴奋不已

你那么美好，克拉克·盖博会为你拜倒

奋不顾身

透过你的假面寻找真我，女孩

不要再有诡雷和炸弹

不要再有堕落和魅惑

不要再有错位的爱，女孩

不要再有肮脏的男人躺在你的臂弯

那个裤子里有鼓槌的百万富翁呢？

他看起来很困惑，很迷惑

当他演奏时，我们没有舞动起来

今晚坚强些，别崩溃
我怕是没法应对
今晚坚强些，别崩溃
昨天不过是回忆
明天永远事与愿违
我需要你，对

Don't Fall Apart on Me Tonight

Just a minute before you leave, girl
Just a minute before you touch the door
What is it that you're trying to achieve, girl?
Do you think we can talk about it some more?
You know, the streets are filled with vipers
Who've lost all ray of hope
You know, it ain't even safe no more
In the palace of the Pope

Don't fall apart on me tonight
I just don't think that I could handle it
Don't fall apart on me tonight
Yesterday's just a memory
Tomorrow is never what it's supposed to be
And I need you, yeah

Come over here from over there, girl
Sit down here. You can have my chair
I can't see us goin' anywhere, girl
The only place open is a thousand miles away and I can't
    take you there
I wish I'd have been a doctor
Maybe I'd have saved some life that had been lost
Maybe I'd have done some good in the world
'Stead of burning every bridge I crossed

Don't fall apart on me tonight
I just don't think that I could handle it
Don't fall apart on me tonight

Yesterday's just a memory
Tomorrow is never what it's supposed to be
And I need you, oh, yeah

I ain't too good at conversation, girl
So you might not know exactly how I feel
But if I could, I'd bring you to the mountaintop, girl
And build you a house made out of stainless steel
But it's like I'm stuck inside a painting
That's hanging in the Louvre
My throat start to tickle and my nose itches
But I know that I can't move

Don't fall apart on me tonight
I just don't think that I could handle it
Don't fall apart on me tonight
Yesterday's gone but the past lives on
Tomorrow's just one step beyond
And I need you, oh, yeah

Who are these people who are walking towards you?
Do you know them or will there be a fight?
With their humorless smiles so easy to see through
Can they tell you what's wrong from what's right?
Do you remember St. James Street
Where you blew Jackie P.'s mind?
You were so fine, Clark Gable would have fell at your feet
And laid his life on the line

Let's try to get beneath the surface waste, girl
No more booby traps and bombs
No more decadence and charm
No more affection that's misplaced, girl

172

No more mudcake creatures lying in your arms
What about that millionaire with the drumsticks in his
    pants?
He looked so baffled and so bewildered
When he played and we didn't dance

Don't fall apart on me tonight
I just don't think that I could handle it
Don't fall apart on me tonight
Yesterday's just a memory
Tomorrow is never what it's supposed to be
And I need you, yeah

盲歌手威利·麦克泰尔[1]

看见门柱上的箭

说："这是片被诅咒的土地

从耶路撒冷

一直到新奥尔良"

我穿越东得克萨斯

众多烈士在那里阵亡

我告诉你一件事

没人能把蓝调唱得

像盲歌手威利·麦克泰尔一样

哦，当他们拆掉帐篷

我听到森鸮在歌唱

枯树上空的星辰

是他仅有的听众

深肤色的吉普赛姑娘

善于炫耀她们的美丽

我告诉你一件事

1.盲歌手威利·麦克泰尔（Blind Willie McTell，1898—1959），影响深远的美国蓝调歌手。迪伦曾在数首歌曲中向他致敬，这首歌便是其中一首。

没人能把蓝调唱得

像盲歌手威利·麦克泰尔一样

河边有个女人

和一个英俊的小伙在一起

他穿得像个乡绅

手握私酿威士忌

有些人战死沙场

有些人死里逃生

我告诉你一件事

没人能把蓝调唱得

像盲歌手威利·麦克泰尔一样

哦，上帝在他的天堂里

我们都想要他的东西

但权力、贪欲和腐败的种子

才是我们这里的全部

我在圣詹姆斯旅馆

凝望着窗外

我告诉你一件事

没人能把蓝调唱得

像盲歌手威利·麦克泰尔一样

Blind Willie McTell

Seen the arrow on the doorpost
Saying, "This land is condemned
All the way from New Orleans
To new Jerusalem"
I traveled through East Texas
Where many martyrs fell
And I can tell you one thing
Nobody can sing the blues
Like Blind Willie McTell

Well, I heard that hoot owl singing
As they were taking down the tents
The stars above the barren trees
Were his only audience
Them charcoal gypsy maidens
Can strut their feathers well
And I can tell you one thing
Nobody can sing the blues
Like Blind Willie McTell

There's a woman by the river
With some fine young handsome man
He's dressed up like a squire
Bootlegged whiskey in his hand
Some of them died in the battle
Some of them survived as well
And I can tell you one thing
Nobody can sing the blues
Like Blind Willie McTell

Well, God is in His heaven
And we all want what's His
But power and greed and corruptible seed
Seem to be all that there is
I'm gazing out the window
Of the St. James Hotel
And I can tell you one thing
Nobody can sing the blues
Like Blind Willie McTell

骄傲的脚 [1]

就像狮子能从男人身上撕下肉

冒充男人的女人也能

他们在他的葬礼上唱《丹尼少年》和主祷文

传教士谈论着耶稣被背叛

就像地面开口将他吞噬 [2]

他爬得太高，被抛回地面

他们说向上爬时，对遇到的好人好点

因为你掉下来时，还会遇到他们

哦，没有回头路

当你骄傲的脚一旦踏出

没有回头路

听说你有个名叫雅各的兄弟，别忘了面孔或名字

脸颊凹陷的混血儿

1.《旧约·诗篇》36:11："不容骄傲人的脚踏我，不容凶恶人的手赶逐我。"

2. 地面开裂吞噬之象，屡见于《圣经》，如《旧约·民数记》16:30 及《旧约·申命记》11:6。

他直视太阳，说复仇在我 [1]

但他喝酒，酒里能下药

再给我唱一首歌，关于你爱我至深和陌生人

还有你和埃罗尔·弗林倒在刀下的风流事儿

这怜悯的时代，遵从成了潮流

在最后一根钉子钉入之前，再跟我讲一件蠢事

哦，没有回头路

当你骄傲的脚一旦踏出

没有回头路

有个名叫雷德的退休商人

被赶下天堂，[2] 他发了疯

从每个能接触到的人那儿榨取养分

他说他只收现金，只售死亡航班的机票

你不经常和他一起厮混

大利拉小姐是他的女人，她就是一俗人 [3]

1.《新约·罗马书》12:19："亲爱的弟兄，不要自己伸冤，宁可让步，听凭主
怒（或作"让人发怒"）。因为经上记着：'主说，伸冤在我，我必报应。'"
2. 雷德，暗示撒旦，基督教中红色代表血、罪、死亡，是上帝用来表示撒旦
的颜色，比如大红龙。《圣经》中撒旦被逐出天堂。
3. 大利拉，参孙情妇，出卖参孙，是非利士人（Philistine）。Philistine 也指
缺乏文化教养的庸俗之辈。迪伦将 Philistine 拼成 Phillistine。

她会奇妙地改变你的命运，在你床头喂你吃椰子面包
    和香料蛋糕
如果你不介意在墓里脸朝下睡觉

哦，没有回头路
当你骄傲的脚一旦踏出
没有回头路

好吧，今晚他们会挑个男人和你见面
你将扮演傻瓜，学习如何穿过大门
如何进入天堂之门
不，是如何挑起一副重得不该你挑的担子
是的，舞台上他们试图击磐石出活水 [1]
一个妓女将募款十万块并说声多谢
他们拿走这些沾着罪恶的钱，建些供人学习的大学
一路唱着《奇异恩典》到瑞士银行

哦，没有回头路
当你骄傲的脚一旦踏出
没有回头路

---

1. 摩西曾两次杖击磐石出水，见《旧约·出埃及记》17:6 及《旧约·民数记》
20:9-11。

他们那儿有漂亮的人儿，老弟

他们会让你心生恐惧，并教你怎么管好自己的嘴

他们的额上写满了奥秘 [1]

他们杀死婴儿床上的婴儿，说只有好人会早死

他们不相信仁慈

他们所遭的天谴你永远看不见

他们歌颂你或打倒你

把你变成他们希望你成为的人

哦，没有回头路

当你骄傲的脚一旦踏出

没有回头路

是的，我想我也爱他

他爬那座山的情景，还在我脑海里

他有没有成功登顶？他可能登顶了又掉下去

被意志的力量击垮

这儿什么都没留下，朋友，仅是瘟疫之灰就让全镇害怕

从现在起，你来自这里

1.《新约·启示录》17:5："在她额上有名写着说：'奥秘哉！大巴比伦，作世上的淫妇和一切可憎之物的母。'"

任凭死人埋葬死人 [1]。你的日子将至

任凭热铁销熔，在他召鬼之时 [2]

哦，没有回头路

当你骄傲的脚一旦踏出

没有回头路

1.《新约·马太福音》8:22："耶稣说：'任凭死人埋葬他们的死人，你跟从我吧！'"

2.《新约·提摩太前书》4:1-2："圣灵明说：在后来的时候，必有人离弃真道，听从那引诱人的邪灵和鬼魔的道理。这是因为说谎之人的假冒，这等人的良心如同被热铁烙惯了一般。"

Foot of Pride

Like the lion tears the flesh off of a man
So can a woman who passes herself off as a male
They sang "Danny Boy" at his funeral and the Lord's Prayer
Preacher talking 'bout Christ betrayed
It's like the earth just opened and swallowed him up
He reached too high, was thrown back to the ground
You know what they say about bein' nice to the right people
   on the way up
Sooner or later you gonna meet them comin' down

Well, there ain't no goin' back
When your foot of pride come down
Ain't no goin' back

Hear ya got a brother named James, don't forget faces or
   names
Sunken cheeks and his blood is mixed
He looked straight into the sun and said revenge is mine
But he drinks, and drinks can be fixed
Sing me one more song, about ya love me to the moon and
   the stranger
And your fall-by-the sword love affair with Errol Flynn
In these times of compassion when conformity's in fashion
Say one more stupid thing to me before the final nail is
   driven in

Well, there ain't no goin' back
When your foot of pride come down
Ain't no goin' back

There's a retired businessman named Red
Cast down from heaven and he's out of his head
He feeds off of everyone that he can touch
He said he only deals in cash or sells tickets to a plane crash
He's not somebody that you play around with much
Miss Delilah is his, a Phillistine is what she is
She'll do wondrous works with your fate, feed you coconut
    bread, spice buns in your bed
If you don't mind sleepin' with your head face down in
    a grave

Well, there ain't no goin' back
When your foot of pride come down
Ain't no goin' back

Well, they'll choose a man for you to meet tonight
You'll play the fool and learn how to walk through doors
How to enter into the gates of paradise
No, how to carry a burden too heavy to be yours
Yeah, from the stage they'll be tryin' to get water outa rocks
A whore will pass the hat, collect a hundred grand and say
    thanks
They like to take all this money from sin, build big
    universities to study in
Sing "Amazing Grace" all the way to the Swiss banks

Well, there ain't no goin' back
When your foot of pride come down
Ain't no goin' back

They got some beautiful people out there, man
They can be a terror to your mind and show you how to
    hold your tongue

They got mystery written all over their forehead
They kill babies in the crib and say only the good die young
They don't believe in mercy
Judgement on them is something that you'll never see
They can exalt you up or bring you down main route
Turn you into anything that they want you to be

Well, there ain't no goin' back
When your foot of pride come down
Ain't no goin' back

Yes, I guess I loved him too
I can still see him in my mind climbin' that hill
Did he make it to the top, well he probably did and dropped
Struck down by the strength of the will
Ain't nothin' left here partner, just the dust of a plague
    that has left this whole town afraid
From now on, this'll be where you're from
Let the dead bury the dead. Your time will come
Let hot iron blow as he raised the shade

Well, there ain't no goin' back
When your foot of pride come down
Ain't no goin' back

主啊，请保护我的孩子

以他的年龄，他很聪明

他遗传了他母亲的眼睛

他心里很高兴

他狂野，他年轻

我唯一的祈祷是，如果我不能在那里

主啊，请保护我的孩子

他的青春开始展开

他已历经几个世纪

只是看他嬉戏，我就笑意盈盈

不管我遭何不测

不管我命运如何

主啊，请保护我的孩子

全世界都在梦乡

你可以看着它哭泣

你找到的东西鲜有重要的

虽然我要的不多

不需要触摸物质的东西

主啊，请保护我的孩子

他血气方刚

充满希望和欲望

在一个被奸污和亵渎的世界

如果我跌倒在路上

再也看不到明天

主啊，请保护我的孩子

我听说终有一天

一切会好

人会跟上帝和解

但在他们失去锁链

正义实现之前

主啊，请保护我的孩子

Lord Protect My Child

For his age, he's wise
He's got his mother's eyes
There's gladness in his heart
He's young and he's wild
My only prayer is, if I can't be there
Lord, protect my child

As his youth now unfolds
He is centuries old
Just to see him at play makes me smile
No matter what happens to me
No matter what my destiny
Lord, protect my child

The whole world is asleep
You can look at it and weep
Few things you find are worthwhile
And though I don't ask for much
No material things to touch
Lord, protect my child

He's young and on fire
Full of hope and desire
In a world that's been raped and defiled
If I fall along the way
And can't see another day
Lord, protect my child

There'll be a time I hear tell

When all will be well
When God and man will be reconciled
But until men lose their chains
And righteousness reigns
Lord, protect my child

有人抓住了我的心

（《与我的心紧密相关》早期版本）

他们说："吃喝快乐吧"[1]

"迎难而上"

我不断看到你的幻影，一朵荆棘中的百合[2]

一切都有点遥不可及

越来越难以识别陷阱

太多无关紧要的信息

太多不再草根的说唱

就像你告诉我的，就像你说的那样

月亮像野火一样升起

我感觉到暴风雨的气息

今晚我得做点什么

你进去，别冻着

有人抓住了我的心

———————

1.《新约·路加福音》12:19："只管安安逸逸地吃喝快乐吧！"

2.《旧约·雅歌》2:2："我的佳偶在女子中，好像百合花在荆棘内。"

有人抓住了我的心

有人抓住了我的心

你——

是的，你抓住了我的心

刚从一座火红天空的城市回来

人人都用胃来思考

间谍多如牛毛

每条街道都弯弯曲曲，兜兜转转到消失无影

蝴蝶夫人哄我入睡

像一条古老的河流

如此宽广而深邃

她说："放轻松，心肝儿，这儿没什么值得偷的"

你是我一直在等的人

你是我渴望得到的人

但你首先得领悟

我不像他们一样可供出租

有人抓住了我的心

有人抓住了我的心

有人抓住了我的心

你，你，你，你

是的，你抓住了我的心

听到热血的歌手

在舞台上轻哼

《九月之歌》《六月里的孟菲斯》

当他们暴揍一个戴粉末蓝假发的男人

我去过巴比伦

我得承认

我仍听得到旷野里的喊声

远看是庞然大物，近看并非硕大无朋

永远学不会把血当酒饮

永远学不会看着你的脸庞说你属于我

有人抓住了我的心

有人抓住了我的心

有人抓住了我的心

你——

是的，你抓住了我的心

Someone's Got a Hold of My Heart
(Early version of "Tight Connection to My Heart")

They say, "Eat, drink and be merry"
"Take the bull by the horns"
I keep seeing visions of you, a lily among thorns
Everything looks a little far away to me

Gettin' harder and harder to recognize the trap
Too much information about nothin'
Too much educated rap
It's just like you told me, just like you said it would be

The moon rising like wildfire
I feel the breath of a storm
Something I got to do tonight
You go inside and stay warm

Someone's got a hold of my heart
Someone's got a hold of my heart
Someone's got a hold of my heart
You—
Yeah, you got a hold of my heart

Just got back from a city of flaming red skies
Everybody thinks with their stomach
There's plenty of spies
Every street is crooked, they just wind around till they
    disappear

Madame Butterfly, she lulled me to sleep

Like an ancient river
So wide and deep
She said, "Be easy, baby, ain't nothin' worth stealin' here"

You're the one I've been waitin' for
You're the one I desire
But you must first realize
I'm not another man for hire

Someone's got a hold of my heart
Someone's got a hold of my heart
Someone's got a hold of my heart
You, you, you, you
Yeah, you got a hold of my heart

Hear that hot-blooded singer
On the bandstand croon
September song, Memphis in June
While they're beating the devil out of a guy who's wearing
    a powder blue wig

I been to Babylon
I gotta confess
I could still hear the voice crying in the wilderness
What looks large from a distance, close up is never that big
Never could learn to drink that blood and call it wine
Never could learn to look at your face and call it mine

Someone's got a hold of my heart
Someone's got a hold of my heart
Someone's got a hold of my heart
You—
Yeah, you got a hold of my heart

告诉我

告诉我——我得知道
告诉我——在我走之前告诉我
火焰是否还在燃烧，火光是否还在闪烁？
抑或已经熄灭，像雪一样融化？
告诉我
告诉我

告诉我——你的聚焦点是什么？
告诉我——你走后它会奔向我？
快使眼色告诉我
我应该抱紧你还是让你走过？
告诉我
告诉我

你看着我却想着别人？
你能感觉到我脉搏的热力和敲击？
你有没有什么秘密
迟早会被人所知
你是否躺在床上凝望星星？
你最重要的朋友是我们的老相识？

告诉我

告诉我

告诉我——那些漂亮的棕色眼睛后面是什么？

告诉我——你的珍宝放在哪扇门背后？

你曾彻底破产过？

曾和专家说的背道而驰？

告诉我

告诉我

你在和我玩某种游戏？

我在想象一件不可能的事？

你有道德吗？

你有观点吗？

我在你脸上看到的是微笑？

它会给你带来耻辱还是荣耀？

告诉我

告诉我

告诉我——我的名字在你的书里？

告诉我——你会回去再看一眼

告诉我真相，别跟我说谎

有人为你哭泣或祈祷？

告诉我

告诉我

Tell Me

Tell me—I've got to know
Tell me—Tell me before I go
Does that flame still burn, does that fire still glow
Or has it died out and melted like the snow
Tell me
Tell me

Tell me—what are you focused upon
Tell me—will it come to me after you're gone
Tell me quick with a glance on the side
Shall I hold you close or shall I let you go by
Tell me
Tell me

Are you lookin' at me and thinking of somebody else
Can you feel the heat and the beat of my pulse
Do you have any secrets
That will only come out in time
Do you lay in bed and stare at the stars
Is your main friend someone who's an old acquaintance of
    ours
Tell me
Tell me

Tell me—what's in back of them pretty brown eyes
Tell me—behind what door your treasure lies
Ever gone broke in a big way
Ever done the opposite of what the experts say
Tell me

Tell me

Is it some kind of game that you're playin' with me
Am I imagining something that never can be
Do you have any morals
Do you have any point of view
Is that a smile I see on your face
Will it take you to glory or to disgrace
Tell me
Tell me

Tell me—is my name in your book
Tell me—will you go back and take another look
Tell me the truth, tell me no lies
Are you someone whom anyone prays for or cries
Tell me
Tell me

(hesitated)
If I'd a thought about, I wouldn't've done it, I think I
                                                        woulda let it slide
If I'd a lived my life by what others ~~think~~ think, the heart
(I'd have asked   inside me would've die
(remembered
but I wished for man's ...... than his cheap morality,
Some one had to reach for the rising star, it looked like it
                                                    was up to me

帝国滑稽剧
Empire Burlesque

李皖　译（郝佳　校）

《帝国滑稽剧》发行于 1985 年 6 月 10 日，是鲍勃·迪伦的第二十三张录音室专辑。因其带有明显的 20 世纪 80 年代"流行风"，铁杆迪伦迷和尖刻的批评家对它评价极低，认为它失去了迪伦以往的风采、风格和水准。

有评论称它为"迪斯科迪伦""平庸的流行歌曲"，也有报道说迪伦试图创造一种"当代声响"。迪伦对此带点儿玩笑地回应说，他对新音乐一无所知，他仍然在听查理·帕顿（Charley Patton，美国 20 世纪二三十年代蓝调歌手）的歌。

这张专辑的一部分歌词受到了严厉批评，另一部分却引起了评论界的浓厚兴趣，尤其是对其奇特乃至古怪的灵感来源，多有挖掘和考据。有的歌词像是好莱坞老电影的对白拼贴；有的歌词像是一些噩兆，表露了作者不祥的预感；有的歌词则像是受到偶然场景的触动，一蹴而就。

从创作过程看，这张专辑经历了特别长的制作周期，特别多的杂事干扰，特别多的团队成员变动，特别多的作品的更改、废弃与再造。

　　以我的观察，这些歌词包括了关联密切、统一的一部分，和相对游离的、与整体无关的一部分。前者是一些特殊的情歌，事关两性间的磕磕绊绊，不乏琐碎，但琐碎中含义丰富，感情真挚强烈，其语言风格、美学面貌在诗史上亦属少有；后者包括《干净整洁的孩子》《信你自己》《黑暗的眼睛》等作品，各自独立，风格鲜明，尤其后两首，一首是迪伦的道德告诫书，一首是语词密集而凝练的意象短诗，具有与典型迪伦风格不同的样貌。

李皖

与我的心紧密相关

（有人见到我的爱人吗）[1]

唉，我得赶紧走了

你搂着我的脖子可不行

我说过我会派人接你并且做到了

你还有什么不满意？

我的手在出汗

可我们还什么都没干

我会继续装模作样下去

直到找到出去的路

我知道这完全是个天大的笑话

不管它到底怎么回事

也许有一天

我会记得忘记

要去拿我的外套

我感觉到暴风雨的气息

今晚我得去办点事

---

1. 这首歌的歌词多处源自电影台词，尤其是鲍嘉主演的电影中的台词。又，《旧约·雅歌》3:3："我问他们：'你们看见我心所爱的没有？'"

你到里面去，别冻着

有人见到我的爱人吗
有人见到我的爱人吗
有人见到我的爱人吗
我不知道
有人见到我的爱人吗？

你想跟我说话
直说吧
无论你要说什么
都不会造成打击
一定是我哪里做错了
你只要对我耳语就好
蝴蝶夫人
她哄我睡觉
在一个没有怜悯的小镇
那里水流深深
她说："放松孩子
这儿没什么值得偷的"

你是我一直要找的人
你是那个有钥匙的人

但我搞不清楚是你配不上我

还是我配不上你

有人见到我的爱人吗

有人见到我的爱人吗

有人见到我的爱人吗

我不知道

有人见到我的爱人吗?

唉，今夜他们没亮出一点儿光

也没有月亮

只有一个热血歌手

在唱着《六月里的孟菲斯》

这时他们正在暴打一个家伙

他戴着淡蓝色的假发

稍后因为拒捕

他将被警察枪杀

我依然能听见他呼喊的声音

在旷野里

离远看很巨大的东西

凑近看却未必

永未能学会饮血

还把它叫作酒

永未能学会抱你，亲爱的

还说你是我的

Tight Connection to My Heart
(Has Anybody Seen My Love)

Well, I had to move fast
And I couldn't with you around my neck
I said I'd send for you and I did
What did you expect?
My hands are sweating
And we haven't even started yet
I'll go along with the charade
Until I can think my way out
I know it was all a big joke
Whatever it was about
Someday maybe
I'll remember to forget

I'm gonna get my coat
I feel the breath of a storm
There's something I've got to do tonight
You go inside and stay warm

Has anybody seen my love
Has anybody seen my love
Has anybody seen my love
I don't know
Has anybody seen my love?

You want to talk to me
Go ahead and talk
Whatever you got to say to me

Won't come as any shock
I must be guilty of something
You just whisper it into my ear
Madame Butterfly
She lulled me to sleep
In a town without pity
Where the water runs deep
She said, "Be easy, baby
There ain't nothin' worth stealin' in here"

You're the one I've been looking for
You're the one that's got the key
But I can't figure out whether I'm too good for you
Or you're too good for me

Has anybody seen my love
Has anybody seen my love
Has anybody seen my love
I don't know
Has anybody seen my love?

Well, they're not showing any lights tonight
And there's no moon
There's just a hot-blooded singer
Singing "Memphis in June"
While they're beatin' the devil out of a guy
Who's wearing a powder-blue wig
Later he'll be shot
For resisting arrest
I can still hear his voice crying
In the wilderness
What looks large from a distance
Close up ain't never that big

Never could learn to drink that blood
And call it wine
Never could learn to hold you, love
And call you mine

终于看见真的你 [1]

哦，我以为雨水会平息一切
可看来它没有
我想让你改变主意
可看来你不会

从现在起我要忙起来了
一时哪儿也去不了
我很高兴事情结束了
而我终于看见真的你

哦，我不曾为你冒生命危险吗
我不曾接受机会的挑战吗？
我不曾摆脱这最不济的逆境吗
全为了你？

哦，我经历过一些糜烂的夜
以为它们永远不会过去

---

1. 这首歌的歌词多处源自电影台词，尤其是鲍嘉主演的电影以及一些西部片
的台词。

现在我只觉得庆幸又感激

得以终于看见真的你

我又饥饿又暴躁

对这些把戏感到厌烦

以前我身上的所有毛病

你都可以医治

哦，我曾把自己绑在桅杆上

穿过了风暴

但那时刻到了

而我终于看见真的你

当我遇见你时，宝贝

你的身上没有可见的疤痕

你会像安妮·奥克利[1]那样骑马

像贝尔·斯塔尔[2]那样射击

哦，我不在乎一定的困难

---

1. 安妮·奥克利（Annie Oakley, 1860—1926），美国"水牛比尔"马戏
团女明星、著名的神枪手、马术师。
2. 贝尔·斯塔尔（Belle Starr, 1848—1889），具有传奇色彩的美国西部女
匪，有"强盗女王"之称。

困难总会过去
但我现在在乎的
是我终于看见真的你

哦，我将停止这孩子气的话
我想我该早一点懂得
我有麻烦，我想也许你也有麻烦
我想也许最好我们各自待着

不管你要做什么
请赶紧做
我依然在努力习惯
终于看见真的你

Seeing the Real You at Last

Well, I thought that the rain would cool things down
But it looks like it don't
I'd like to get you to change your mind
But it looks like you won't

From now on I'll be busy
Ain't goin' nowhere fast
I'm just glad it's over
And I'm seeing the real you at last

Well, didn't I risk my neck for you
Didn't I take chances?
Didn't I rise above it all for you
The most unfortunate circumstances?

Well, I have had some rotten nights
Didn't think that they would pass
I'm just thankful and grateful
To be seeing the real you at last

I'm hungry and I'm irritable
And I'm tired of this bag of tricks
At one time there was nothing wrong with me
That you could not fix

Well, I sailed through the storm
Strapped to the mast
But the time has come
And I'm seeing the real you at last

When I met you, baby
You didn't show no visible scars
You could ride like Annie Oakley
You could shoot like Belle Starr

Well, I don't mind a reasonable amount of trouble
Trouble always comes to pass
But all I care about now
Is that I'm seeing the real you at last

Well, I'm gonna quit this baby talk now
I guess I should have known
I got troubles, I think maybe you got troubles
I think maybe we'd better leave each other alone

Whatever you gonna do
Please do it fast
I'm still trying to get used to
Seeing the real you at last

我会记得你

我会记得你

当我把别的一切都忘记

你对我是真实

你对我是第一

当一切都已不再

你切入了核心

比我知道的任何人都快

当我孤身一人

在巨大的未知中

我会记得你

我会记得你

在小路的尽头

那么多的事情要做

那么少的时间可以失败

有一些人

你没有忘记

即便你只见过他们一两次

当玫瑰凋落

而我在阴影中

我会记得你

我有没有，我有没有努力地爱你？
我有没有，我有没有努力地珍惜？
我有没有在你身旁睡去、哭泣
当那雨水，吹进你的发丝？

我会记得你
当风吹过松林
是你径直走来
是你懂得
虽然我决不会说
我的所作所为
都如你期许
最后
我亲爱的甜蜜的朋友
我会记得你

I'll Remember You

I'll remember you
When I've forgotten all the rest
You to me were true
You to me were the best
When there is no more
You cut to the core
Quicker than anyone I knew
When I'm all alone
In the great unknown
I'll remember you

I'll remember you
At the end of the trail
I had so much left to do
I had so little time to fail
There's some people that
You don't forget
Even though you've only seen 'm one time or two
When the roses fade
And I'm in the shade
I'll remember you

Didn't I, didn't I try to love you?
Didn't I, didn't I try to care?
Didn't I sleep, didn't I weep beside you
With the rain blowing in your hair?

I'll remember you
When the wind blows through the piney wood

It was you who came right through
It was you who understood
Though I'd never say
That I done it the way
That you'd have liked me to
In the end
My dear sweet friend
I'll remember you

干净整洁的孩子 [1]

每个人都纳闷为什么他不能适应

适应什么？一个破碎的梦？

他是一个干净整洁的孩子

他们却把他变成了一个杀手

这就是他们干的事

他们说上就是下，他们说不是就是是

他们把思想灌进他脑子，他以为是他想的

他是一个干净整洁的孩子

他们却把他变成了一个杀手

这就是他们干的事

他在棒球队，他在仪仗队

他在十岁的时候有了一个西瓜摊

---

1. 这首歌的歌词讲述了普通的美国年轻人在越战中经历的剧烈改变，美国乐评人罗伯特·克里斯戈（Robert Christgau）称之为"迄今最尖锐的越战老兵之歌"。

他是一个干净整洁的孩子
他们却把他变成了一个杀手
这就是他们干的事

他礼拜天去教堂，他是一名童子军
为朋友他会把口袋翻个里朝外

他是一个干净整洁的孩子
他们却把他变成了一个杀手
这就是他们干的事

他们说："听着小子，你还太嫩"
他们送他到汽油弹保健水疗地成长

他们给他大麻抽，给酒和药丸
给他吉普开，让鲜血四溅

他们说："祝贺你，你通过了"
他们把他送回竞争，不带任何刹车

他是一个干净整洁的孩子
他们却把他变成了一个杀手
这就是他们干的事

他买了美国梦，可这让他负债累累

他唯一能玩的游戏，是俄罗斯轮盘赌

他喝可口可乐，吃奇迹牌面包

食汉堡王，吃得可真不赖

他去好莱坞，看彼得·奥图尔[1]

他偷了辆劳斯莱斯，开进了游泳池

他们把一个干净整洁的孩子

变成了一个杀手

这就是他们干的事

他本可卖保险，拥有一家餐厅或酒吧

本可成为会计或网球明星

他戴着拳套，有一天佯作被击倒

从金门大桥，扎进了中国湾

他的妈妈踱来踱去，爸爸流泪呻吟

---

1. 彼得·奥图尔（Peter O'Toole，1932—2013），英国男演员，因主演《阿拉伯的劳伦斯》（*Lawrence of Arabia*，1962）而驰名国际。

他们得一起睡在一个不属于自己的家

他们把一个干净整洁的孩子
变成了一个杀手
这就是他们干的事

呃，每一个人都问他为什么不能适应
而他需要的只是，一个可以信任的人

他们把他的脑袋翻了个里朝外
他永远都不知道，这一切是怎么回事

他有了一份稳定的工作，他加入了唱诗班
他从未打算在高空中走索

他们把一个干净整洁的孩子
变成了一个杀手
这就是他们干的事

Clean-Cut Kid

Everybody wants to know why he couldn't adjust
Adjust to what, a dream that bust?

He was a clean-cut kid
But they made a killer out of him
That's what they did

They said what's up is down, they said what isn't is
They put ideas in his head he thought were his

He was a clean-cut kid
But they made a killer out of him
That's what they did

He was on the baseball team, he was in the marching band
When he was ten years old he had a watermelon stand

He was a clean-cut kid
But they made a killer out of him
That's what they did

He went to church on Sunday, he was a Boy Scout
For his friends he would turn his pockets inside out

He was a clean-cut kid
But they made a killer out of him
That's what they did

They said, "Listen boy, you're just a pup"

They sent him to a napalm health spa to shape up

They gave him dope to smoke, drinks and pills
A jeep to drive, blood to spill

They said "Congratulations, you got what it takes"
They sent him back into the rat race without any brakes

He was a clean-cut kid
But they made a killer out of him
That's what they did

He bought the American dream but it put him in debt
The only game he could play was Russian roulette

He drank Coca-Cola, he was eating Wonder Bread
Ate Burger Kings, he was well fed

He went to Hollywood to see Peter O'Toole
He stole a Rolls-Royce and drove it in a swimming pool

They took a clean-cut kid
And they made a killer out of him
That's what they did

He could've sold insurance, owned a restaurant or bar
Could've been an accountant or a tennis star

He was wearing boxing gloves, took a dive one day
Off the Golden Gate Bridge into China Bay

His mama walks the floor, his daddy weeps and moans
They gotta sleep together in a home they don't own

They took a clean-cut kid
And they made a killer out of him
That's what they did

Well, everybody's asking why he couldn't adjust
All he ever wanted was somebody to trust

They took his head and turned it inside out
He never did know what it was all about

He had a steady job, he joined the choir
He never did plan to walk the high wire

They took a clean-cut kid
And they made a killer out of him
That's what they did

永远不一样了

你现在在我身边，宝贝
你是一个栩栩如生的梦
每一次你离我这么近
都让我想要尖叫
你抚摸我并且知道
我为你而激动，然后
我将永远不一样了

抱歉若我伤了你，宝贝
抱歉若真是如此
抱歉若我触及
你隐藏秘密之地
但你的意义超过一切
而我不能假装
我将永远不一样了

每一次见面，宝贝
你都令我有所思量
别担心宝贝，我不在意离去
我只是希望那是我自己的主意

你教我如何爱你，宝贝

你教我，啊，教得多么好

如今，我无法恢复原状了，宝贝

我不能让钟声倒回去

你拿走了我的现实

把它掷向风

而我将永远不一样了

Never Gonna Be the Same Again

Now you're here beside me, baby
You're a living dream
And every time you get this close
It makes me want to scream
You touched me and you knew
That I was warm for you and then
I ain't never gonna be the same again

Sorry if I hurt you, baby
Sorry if I did
Sorry if I touched the place
Where your secrets are hid
But you meant more than everything
And I could not pretend
I ain't never gonna be the same again

You give me something to think about, baby
Every time I see ya
Don't worry, baby, I don't mind leaving
I'd just like it to be my idea

You taught me how to love you, baby
You taught me, oh, so well
Now, I can't go back to what was, baby
I can't unring the bell
You took my reality
And cast it to the wind
And I ain't never gonna be the same again

信你自己

信你自己
信你自己去做只有你最了解的事
信你自己
信你自己会做正确的事无可指摘
不要信我会给你展示美
既然美可能只会生锈
如果你需要信什么人，信你自己

信你自己
信你自己会知晓终可证明为真之道
信你自己
信你自己找得到那没有"如果""既然"的途径
不要信我会给你呈现真理
既然真理可能只是尘与灰
如果你需要信什么人，信你自己

是啊，你独自一人，你一直如此
在群狼与众贼之地 [1]

1.《新约·约翰福音》10:1-12，耶稣以羊圈作比喻时，视狼和贼为羊之大敌，
羊喻基督教徒。

别把希望寄托于不敬虔的人
也不要做他人之信的奴隶

信你自己
由此再不会为无谓的人让你失望而沮丧
信你自己
由此不再寻找答案在找不到答案的地方
不要信我会让你看到爱
既然我的爱可能只是欲望
如果你需要信什么人，信你自己

Trust Yourself

Trust yourself
Trust yourself to do the things that only you know best
Trust yourself
Trust yourself to do what's right and not be second-guessed
Don't trust me to show you beauty
When beauty may only turn to rust
If you need somebody you can trust, trust yourself

Trust yourself
Trust yourself to know the way that will prove true in the end
Trust yourself
Trust yourself to find the path where there is no if and when
Don't trust me to show you the truth
When the truth may only be ashes and dust
If you want somebody you can trust, trust yourself

Well, you're on your own, you always were
In a land of wolves and thieves
Don't put your hope in ungodly man
Or be a slave to what somebody else believes

Trust yourself
And you won't be disappointed when vain people let you
    down
Trust yourself
And look not for answers where no answers can be found
Don't trust me to show you love
When my love may be only lust
If you want somebody you can trust, trust yourself

充满感情的，你的 [1]

来宝贝来找我，来宝贝提醒我，我是从哪儿开始的
来宝贝向我表明，向我表明你了解我，告诉我你就是
    那一个
我也许在学着，你也许在向往，看到紧闭门后的事
而我将永远是充满感情的，你的

来宝贝摇晃我，来宝贝锁上我，把我锁进你的心影
来宝贝教导我，来宝贝抓住我，让那音乐现在开始
我也许在做梦，但一直都相信，你是我一生所求之人
而我将永远是充满感情的，你的

就好像我的一生从没有发生
当我看见你，就好像我从没有过想法
我知道这个梦，它也许太疯狂
但这是我做过的唯一一个

来宝贝晃动我，来宝贝带上我，我将会感到多么满意

---

1. 歌名及歌词 "emotionally yours"，采用了英文书信的落款格式。为与
歌韵、节奏相协调，拙译如此。

234

来宝贝抱紧我，来宝贝帮助我，我的双臂张得那么辽阔

我不会再迷乱了，不管走到哪里，哪怕到了异国海岸

而我将永远是充满感情的，你的

Emotionally Yours

Come baby, find me, come baby, remind me of where I
   once begun
Come baby, show me, show me you know me, tell me
   you're the one
I could be learning, you could be yearning to see behind
   closed doors
But I will always be emotionally yours

Come baby, rock me, come baby, lock me into the shadows
   of your heart
Come baby, teach me, come baby, reach me, let the music
   start
I could be dreaming but I keep believing you're the one I'm
   livin' for
And I will always be emotionally yours

It's like my whole life never happened
When I see you, it's as if I never had a thought
I know this dream, it might be crazy
But it's the only one I've got

Come baby, shake me, come baby, take me, I would be
   satisfied
Come baby, hold me, come baby, help me, my arms are
   open wide
I could be unraveling wherever I'm traveling, even to foreign
   shores
But I will always be emotionally yours

当黑夜从天空落下

眺望田野，看见我回来
烟雾在你眼中，你露出一丝微笑
壁炉里，我给你的信在燃烧
你有了些时间，好好琢磨了这事

啊，我走了两百英里，瞧我
那追逐结束了，月亮高高悬起
谁爱谁都没关系
你会爱我，或者我会爱你
当黑夜从天空落下

我能看穿你的壁垒，知道你很受伤
悲哀正像斗篷，盖在你身上
直到昨天我才知道
你一直在与灾难周旋嬉戏，设法逃离

我无法提供给你，简单的答案
你是什么人，我何必向你撒谎？
关于这点你终会明白，爱人
它会贴合你像一只手套

当黑夜从天空落下

我能听见你颤抖的心跳像一条河
上次我打电话，你必定是在护着谁
我从没要过你不能付出的东西
我从没要求你作茧自缚

我见过成千上万的人，他们本可战胜黑暗
却因为舍不下一两块臭钱，我看着他们死去
别离开我宝贝，我们还没完蛋
不要寻找我，我会看见你
当黑夜从天空落下

在你的泪珠中，我能看见自己的映像
那是得克萨斯的北界，在那儿我穿过了边境线
我不想做一个渴望爱情的傻瓜
我不想耽溺于别人的酒

永远永远，我想我会记住
那在你眼中咆哮的寒风
你将寻找我并且将寻见
我就在你心灵的荒原中
当黑夜从天空落下

哦，我将感情放在一封信里寄给你
可你在赌的是支持
明天此时我将进一步认清你
到时我的记性不会这么差

这回我会索要自由
从你否定的世界里索要自由
而你一定要给我
不管怎样我一定会得到
当黑夜从天空落下

When the Night Comes Falling from the Sky

Look out across the fields, see me returning
Smoke is in your eye, you draw a smile
From the fireplace where my letters to you are burning
You've had time to think about it for a while

Well, I've walked two hundred miles, now look me over
It's the end of the chase and the moon is high
It won't matter who loves who
You'll love me or I'll love you
When the night comes falling from the sky

I can see through your walls and I know you're hurting
Sorrow covers you up like a cape
Only yesterday I know that you've been flirting
With disaster that you managed to escape

I can't provide for you no easy answers
Who are you that I should have to lie?
You'll know all about it, love
It'll fit you like a glove
When the night comes falling from the sky

I can hear your trembling heart beat like a river
You must have been protecting someone last time I called
I've never asked you for nothing you couldn't deliver
I've never asked you to set yourself up for a fall

I saw thousands who could have overcome the darkness

For the love of a lousy buck, I've watched them die
Stick around, baby, we're not through
Don't look for me, I'll see you
When the night comes falling from the sky

In your teardrops, I can see my own reflection
It was on the northern border of Texas where I crossed the
line
I don't want to be a fool starving for affection
I don't want to drown in someone else's wine

For all eternity I think I will remember
That icy wind that's howling in your eye
You will seek me and you'll find me
In the wasteland of your mind
When the night comes falling from the sky

Well, I sent you my feelings in a letter
But you were gambling for support
This time tomorrow I'll know you better
When my memory is not so short

This time I'm asking for freedom
Freedom from a world which you deny
And you'll give it to me now
I'll take it anyhow
When the night comes falling from the sky

什么东西着了，宝贝

什么东西着了宝贝，你感觉到没有？
出事儿了宝贝，你的头发在冒烟
你还是我朋友吗宝贝，给我个表示
你心里对我的爱是否正变得茫然？

你避开那些大街已经很久很久
我要找的真相在你的遗失档案中
你是什么看法宝贝，到底发生了什么？
你眼中的光何以几近黯淡？

我熟知这个地方的一切，或者看来如此
我不再是你计划或梦想的一部分了？
好吧，很显然事情已经起了变化
发生了什么宝贝，你的举止变得如此陌生？

什么东西着了宝贝，这就是我要说的
即便伦敦的寻血猎犬[1]今天也找不到你

---

1. 寻血猎犬，以辨别人类气味著称，19 世纪始在英国用于缉私。

我看见一个人的阴影宝贝，那让你变得忧郁

他是谁宝贝，他对你意味着什么？

我们已到达道路的边缘宝贝，从那头起就是草场

在那头据说爱可以遮掩许多的罪 [1]

但是你住哪宝贝，灯在哪？

为什么你的眼睛直在黑夜中瞪着

我能在黑夜中感觉到，当我想起你

我能在光芒中感觉到，而这定会成真

你不能单靠面包活着，那样子你不会满意

你不能让石头滚开如果你的双手被捆着

总要起个头的宝贝，你能不能解释一下？

请不要从我身边消失宝贝，仿佛那午夜列车

回答我啊宝贝，随便一个眼神都可以

究竟是什么攫住了你？

我能在风中感觉到，它在翻覆

1.《新约·彼得前书》4:8："最要紧的是彼此切实相爱，因为爱能遮掩许多的罪。"

我能在尘土中感觉到，当我在城镇郊外[1]步下客车
从上一个急转弯起我就有了这墨西哥城蓝调[2]
我不想看你流血，我知道你要什么但这并非你应得

什么东西着了宝贝，有什么东西在火里
有一个人正在到处骂大街
你准备好了就打电话下来宝贝，我在等你
我相信不可能的事，你知道我真的相信

---

1. 城镇郊外，美国歌手路易斯·乔丹（Louis Jordan）有蓝调歌曲《我要搬到城镇郊外》（*I'm Gonna Move to the Outskirts of Town*）及《我要在城镇郊外离开你》（*I'm Gonna Leave You on the Outskirts of Town*），与下句的"蓝调"呼应。
2. 墨西哥城蓝调，杰克·凯鲁亚克于 1959 年创作同名诗歌集。迪伦认为该诗歌集是第一本用美式语言对他说话的书。

Something's Burning, Baby

Something is burning, baby, are you aware?
Something is the matter, baby, there's smoke in your hair
Are you still my friend, baby, show me a sign
Is the love in your heart for me turning blind?

You've been avoiding the main streets for a long, long while
The truth that I'm seeking is in your missing file
What's your position, baby, what's going on?
Why is the light in your eyes nearly gone?

I know everything about this place, or so it seems
Am I no longer a part of your plans or your dreams?
Well, it is so obvious that something has changed
What's happening, baby, to make you act so strange?

Something is burning, baby, here's what I say
Even the bloodhounds of London couldn't find you today
I see the shadow of a man, baby, makin' you blue
Who is he, baby, and what's he to you?

We've reached the edge of the road, baby, where the pasture
   begins
Where charity is supposed to cover up a multitude of sins
But where do you live, baby, and where is the light?
Why are your eyes just staring off in the night?

I can feel it in the night when I think of you
I can feel it in the light and it's got to be true
You can't live by bread alone, you won't be satisfied

You can't roll away the stone if your hands are tied

Got to start someplace, baby, can you explain?
Please don't fade away on me, baby, like the midnight train
Answer me, baby, a casual look will do
Just what in the world has come over you?

I can feel it in the wind and it's upside down
I can feel it in the dust as I get off the bus on the outskirts
    of town
I've had the Mexico City blues since the last hairpin curve
I don't wanna see you bleed, I know what you need but it
    ain't what you deserve

Something is burning, baby, something's in flames
There's a man going 'round calling names
Ring down when you're ready, baby, I'm waiting for you
I believe in the impossible, you know that I do

黑暗的眼睛 [1]

哦，绅士们在交谈，午夜的月亮挂在河边
他们喝完了闲走着这正是我溜走的时机
我住在另一个世界那里生与死被熟记
那里地球和情人的珍珠串在一起我看见的全是黑暗的眼睛

远处传来了鸡鸣，又一个士兵在深深祷告
有个孩子走入迷途，他的母亲哪儿也找不到他了
但我能听见又一面鼓为了让死者复活而敲
当他们走来野兽惊惧我看见的全是黑暗的眼睛

他们告诫我对一切预定目标都要深思熟虑
他们告诫我复仇是甜蜜的，从他们的角度看当然如此
但我对他们的游戏毫无感觉，那里美变得不可辨认
我感到的只是热和火我看见的全是黑暗的眼睛

哦，法兰西女郎上了天堂，一个醉汉掌着方向盘

---

1. 据迪伦的自传和早期访谈，这首歌曲创作灵感源自迪伦半夜步出位于曼哈顿的酒店电梯时，看到一个应召女郎在过道上走来，"……她有着蓝色的眼影，黑色的眼线，深色（黑暗）的眼睛"。

为速度与钢铁的坠落之神饥饿付出了沉重代价

哦，时间短促日子甜蜜激情统治着飞矢

一百万张脸在我脚下我看见的全是黑暗的眼睛

Dark Eyes

Oh, the gentlemen are talking and the midnight moon is on
the riverside
They're drinking up and walking and it is time for me to
slide
I live in another world where life and death are memorized
Where the earth is strung with lovers' pearls and all I see are
dark eyes

A cock is crowing far away and another soldier's deep in prayer
Some mother's child has gone astray, she can't find him
anywhere
But I can hear another drum beating for the dead that rise
Whom nature's beast fears as they come and all I see are
dark eyes

They tell me to be discreet for all intended purposes
They tell me revenge is sweet and from where they stand, I'm
sure it is
But I feel nothing for their game where beauty goes
unrecognized
All I feel is heat and flame and all I see are dark eyes

Oh, the French girl, she's in paradise and a drunken man is
at the wheel
Hunger pays a heavy price to the falling gods of speed and
steel
Oh, time is short and the days are sweet and passion rules
the arrow that flies
A million faces at my feet but all I see are dark eyes